VENUS CAPRICCIO

Volume 3 **By Mai Nishikata**

CONTENTS

カプリチオ
ヴィーナス綺想曲
VENUS
CaPRICCIO
Phrase.12

カプリチオ
ヴィーナス綺想曲
VENUS CAPRICCIO

JOHOKU HIGH SCHOOL
THOSE OF YOU WHO ARE SINGING THE SOPRANO PART...
...PLEASE DO IT...
...WITH MORE FEELING.
TRY TO SING SO THAT YOUR VOICES WILL REACH THE BACK OF THE HALL.
MUSIC ROOM

IN CASE YOU'RE WONDERING WHY AKIRA, A JUNIOR HIGH SCHOOL STUDENT...
LET'S TAKE IT FROM THE TOP ONE MORE TIME.
YES.
MUCH BETTER.
OKAY.
TAKAMI-SAN!
KYAAA
AKIRA-KUN ♡
PIPE DOWN!! NO GROUPIES ALLOWED IN HERE!!
WHAT ARE YOU SO HIGH AND MIGHTY ABOUT? THIS IS JUST THE CHORUS!!
KYAAA! TAKAMI-SAN ♡
...IS WAVING A CONDUCTOR'S STICK AROUND AT MY HIGH SCHOOL, WELL...
GYAAA GYAAA
EH?!
ONE WEEK EARLIER
Y-YOU WANT ME TO PLAY THE PIANO?

YEAH! ♡
WE HEARD YOU WON AN AWARD AT A PIANO COMPETITION RECENTLY, HABARA-SAN!
CAN WE COUNT ON YOU?
TH-THIS IS KIND OF SUDDEN...
NO, IT'S NOT!
YOU'VE GOT A MONTH!
EXACTLY!
P-PLEASE...
PLAY FOR US...!
JOHOKU CHORUS MEMBERS
YAMADA VICE PRESIDENT (2ND YEAR)
MICHINARI PRESIDENT (3RD YEAR)
EIKO MEMBER (3RD YEAR)
MMMM...
......
GRIN GRIN GRIN
ONE DAY, I WAS ASKED TO ACCOMPANY THE CHORUS.
ACTUALLY, THEY...
...ALWAYS BORROWED THE SCHOOL GYM AT THE SAME TIME EVERY YEAR TO GIVE A PERFORMANCE.
BUT BECAUSE THEIR AUDIENCE HAS BEEN DWINDLING BY THE YEAR...
...IT SEEMS THAT THIS TIME AROUND, THEY WERE TOLD BY THE SCHOOL...
...THAT IF A CERTAIN NUMBER OF PEOPLE DIDN'T SHOW UP AT THE PERFORMANCE...
...THEY WOULDN'T BE ABLE TO USE THE GYM FROM NEXT YEAR ON.
WE PUT A LOT OF THOUGHT INTO IT...
...AND FINALLY DECIDED THAT NOT ONLY SHOULD WE UP OUR GAME AS SINGERS...
...BUT ALSO TRY TO GIVE THE STAGE A LITTLE MORE PIZZAZZ.

"PIZZAZZ"?
What is that?
A kind of flower?
NO, IT'S, YOU KNOW, SOMETHING EXCITING, WITH STYLE!!
LIKE A PERFORMANCE WITH THE WINNERS OF THAT PRINCE AND PRINCESS CONTEST!!
* SEE VOLUME 1
FWISH!!
WE'D HAVE TO DOUBLE THE AUDIENCE WITH THAT, FOR SURE!!
EH? "WINNERS"... YOU MEAN AKIRA, TOO?
SURE
YEP! IF IT'S AT ALL POSSIBLE, WE WANT HIM TO CONDUCT US!
WE HEARD HE'S AN OLD FRIEND OF YOURS...
...BUT WHAT DO YOU THINK? YOU TWO, TOGETHER AGAIN ON STAGE...?
UMM...
AKIRA, HUH? I DUNNO...
GASP
Y-YOU'RE ALREADY ASSUMING THAT I'M GONNA DO IT?
CAN WE?
...I REALLY DON'T THINK I CAN. I MEAN, TOO MUCH IS RIDING ON IT FOR YOU GUYS TO LET ME...
I-I'M REALLY SORRY WE SPRANG THIS ON YOU...
ALWAYS REFUSES TO ACCOMPANY INTRAMURAL CHORUS COMPETITIONS, TOO, BECAUSE OF STAGE FRIGHT
...BUT FOR SENIORS LIKE MICHINARI-SAN AND ME, THIS WILL BE OUR LAST CONCERT.
THAT'S WHY WE'RE DYING TO MAKE IT A SUCCESS...

I...
I DON'T WANT IT TO BE THE CHORUS'S LAST CONCERT.
EIKO ...
I KNOW OUR SINGING NEEDS TO BECOME WAY MORE POLISHED...BUT ALSO THE PIANO...
T...
TAKAMI-SAN...
PLEASE...
...WOULD YOU ACCOMPANY US...?
......
SCRATCH
SCRATCH
...YEAH, SURE.
YESSS!
WAHOOO!
AND THAT'S HOW...
If they'd be satisfied with me...
Eh? You'll do it?
Uh-huh. (You're gonna be there, too, so...)
I'M AKIRA SASAKI.
I'LL DO THE BEST I CAN TO HELP YOU.
...AKIRA AND I...

AKIRA, IN THE... FLESH! UNGH!
SPLURT
KYAAA!
BUZZ
W-W-WE'RE HONORED TO HAVE YOU HERE!
BUZZ
I-IT'S A PLEASURE TO MEET YOU!
PRESIDENT
Wow, he's popular...
Totally...
VICE-PREZ
T...
TAKAMI-SAN!
LET'S GIVE THIS OUR ALL!
Somebody, a tissue!
...YEAH.
MUSIC ROOM
...CAME TO HELP THE JOHOKU CHORUS CLUB.
JUST THINK!
BECAUSE OF THIS PROMOTIONAL POSTER...
DUN
TENTH ANNUAL CHORUS CLUB CONCERT
FEATURING
PERFORMING WITH THE CHORUS!
THE RETURN OF THAT PRINCE-PRINCESS CONTEST COMBO!!
DUN
...ALL OF THE NUMBERED SEATS (FREE) WERE SNAPPED UP!!
S-SERIOUSLY?!
FOR REAL! I REALLY APPRECIATE THIS!
I BETTER MAKE SURE THERE ARE TONS OF CHAIRS IN THE GYM THAT NIGHT!!
THAT'S SOME POSTER...
FWAP
GRAB
Ah!
That's not fair!

1

HELLO.
I'M NISHIKATA.

THIS IS VOLUME THREE OF VENUS CAPRICCIO. WOW...VOLUME THREE!!

ON THE COVER OF THIS VOLUME, WE'VE GOT THREE PEOPLE TOGETHER FOR THE FIRST TIME. ACTUALLY, AT THIS STAGE, I GET TO DECIDE THE COLOR OF THE BORDER AND THE COLOR WITHIN THE BORDER.

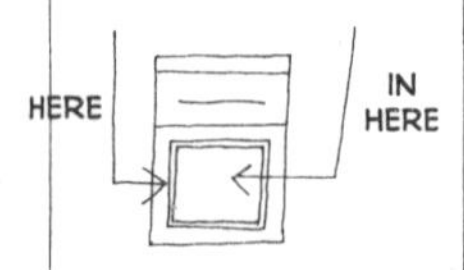

WHAT COLORS SHOULD I CHOOSE...?

THE ILLUSTRATION IS ALREADY FINISHED, SO I WANT THE COLORS TO MATCH UP, BUT NO COLORS ARE COMING TO MIND THAT WOULD GO WELL WITH IT. MAYBE I'LL JUST USE THE SAME COLOR SCHEME THAT I HAD WITH VOLUME ONE.

TELL ME, WHAT COLORS DID I FINALLY GO WITH? HAHAHA.

WELL, I HOPE YOU ENJOY VOLUME THREE OF VENUS!

<- GO!

IT'S ALL THANKS TO YOU TWO!!

UM... THIS IS A LITTLE CLOSE...

ALL RIGHT, BREAK'S OVER...

LET'S GET BACK TO PRACTIC-ING!!

HE'S NOT LISTEN-ING...

YEAHHHH!

HEY, HAVE YOU HEARD ABOUT THE CHORUS CLUB?
TWO WEEKS LATER
YOU MEAN THEIR CONCERT?
I HEARD THEY'RE PRETTY GOOD SINGERS.
ME TOO... AT FIRST, I WAS DRAWN BY THOSE TWO FROM THE PRINCE-PRINCESS CONTEST...
...BUT I'M KIND OF LOOKING FORWARD TO HEARING THE SONGS, TOO.
YEAH, RIGHT?
ARE THEY IN THERE?
MUSIC ROOM
AH! I SEE THEM!
KYAAA ♡
TAKA-MI-SAN! AKIRA-KUN ♡
AGAIN?! JEEZ!
SHUT UP ALREADY!! BEGONE, GROUPIE GIRLS !! LEAVE THAT DOOR SHUT!
COOL IT, COOL IT...
PREZ
HUH? THEY'RE NOT SINGING YET?
AH! THEY'RE PROBABLY JUST GETTING READY TO START.
POP
EXCUSE ME. DO YOU MIND IF WE SIT IN?
DO WHAT?
AH ...
ER ...
GO AHEAD ...
♡ WAAA! THANK YOU!

GREAT JOB, EVERYONE!
Ahaha
ESPECIALLY YOU, HABARA-KUN!
ULP!
GRIN
TWITCH
GRAB
UM... YOU'RE IN TOO CLOSE AGAIN!!
MICHINARI-SAN, THAT'S SEXUAL HARASSMENT RIGHT, AKIRA-KUN?
UH-HUH. NO HESITATION.
UGH! A JUNIOR HIGH SCHOOL STUDENT ACCUSED ME OF SEXUAL HARASSMENT!
THEN LET GO OF ME, PLEASE...
SHEESH...
FWISH
...MM?
STARE
AH! SORRY! I'LL GET THIS CLEANED UP RIGHT AWAY!
TATA
TWITCH
HUH?
AH!
NO...
THAT'S NOT WHAT I WAS...

WHAT?
AH!
P-PARDON ME. IT WAS NOTHING.
GOOD-BYE.
BOW BOW BOW
...?
Y'KNOW ...
...THIS IS THE FIRST TIME I'VE ACCOMPANIED THE CHORUS...
...BUT IT'S ACTUALLY KINDA FUN!
I MEAN, I HAD MY DOUBTS. SINCE PLAYING WITH PEOPLE IS MY WEAK POINT...
...I THOUGHT "WHAT HAPPENS IF IT'S JUST A WASHOUT?"
BUT GETTING IN TUNE WITH THEM...
...I'M HAVING A BLAST!
...
I HOPE...
...THE ACTUAL PERFORMANCE GOES WELL.

GOT THAT RIGHT...
...TAKAMI? WHAT IS IT?
...I JUST REMEMBERED SOMETHING...
RUSTLE RUSTLE
AH! I'LL GO WITH YOU.
NO, THAT'S OKAY. YOU GO AHEAD. I'LL CATCH UP!
I wasn't done talking...
OH, CRAP! I FORGOT THE SCORE.
I'M GONNA GO GET IT.
TA TA TA TA
...HUH?
THIS IS...
...THE PIANO PIECE...
...FOR THE CHORUS.

EIKO-
SAN...?
...SHE'S
GOOD...
...BUT
WHY...
...IS
EIKO-
SAN...?
GOOD,
ISN'T
SHE?
EEEEEEY-
AAAH!
SHUDDER
RATTLE
UH...
...H-HI!
I, UH...
FORGOT
THE
SCORE...
RATTLE
EXCUSE
ME!
EH?
UM...
WHIZZZ

Y--
YOU'RE VERY GOOD.
TWITCH
I-I WAS SURPRISED!
I...
I'M SORRY.
UM... BUT, UH...
YOU'RE MUCH BETTER, TAKAMI-SAN.
MUCH, MUCH BETTER ...
SO...
....
TA TA TA TA
HEY!
EIKO WAS PLAYING?

UH-HUH.
AND SHE WAS GREAT.
YEAH, EIKO USUALLY ACCOMPANIES ...
...BUT THIS TIME I MADE HER A SOPRANO.
PREZ
EH? SHE'S THE ACCOMPANIST?!
WAS, YEAH.
BEEP
I SEE. SO THE CHORUS...
ALREADY HAD AN ACCOMPANIST...
HMM...
STARE
FOR SENIORS LIKE MICHINARI-SAN AND ME, THIS WILL BE OUR LAST CONCERT.
THAT'S WHY WE'RE DYING TO MAKE IT A SUCCESS ...
OH...
I GET IT.
EIKO-SAN...

EIKO-SAN ACTUALLY WANTS TO...
THE DAY OF THE CONCERT...
EHHH?!
WE CAN'T GET TICKETS AT THE DOOR?
BUZZ
BUZZ
S-SORRY. I'M AFRAID WE'RE ALL OUT.

UM... I PUT DOWN MORE CHAIRS, SO GO ON IN.
M-MICHINARI-SAN, ARE YOU SURE?
AND THEY'RE FREE.
WAAA! THANK YOU!
MUSIC ROOM
MORE CHAIRS, HE SAID!
WE HAVEN'T NEEDED THAT BEFORE!
ISN'T HABARA-SAN HERE YET?
NO! WHAT SHOULD WE DO?
WITHOUT HER, WE CAN'T DO A FINAL TUNE UP!
EXCUSE ME!!
AH!
BUZZ
BUZZ

HABARA-SAN, YOU'RE LATE!!
S... SORRY ABOUT THAT.
I HAD A LITTLE ACCIDENT...
YEAH, YEAH. NEVER MIND THE EXCUSES. LET'S START OUR LAST TUNING UP.
WE'VE ONLY GOT A LITTLE WHILE BEFORE THE SHOW STARTS.
...UM...
MM? WHAT'S WRONG?
TAKAMI?
...ACTU-ALLY...
!! !!
TH-THIS MORN-ING I FELL...
...AND SPRAIN-ED MY WRIST...
BOW BOW
BOW
I AM SO SORRY!!

BUZZ
W-WHAT'RE WE GONNA DO?!
THE CONCERT STARTS IN A LITTLE BIT...
I KNOW! I'M SORRY!
EHHH?!
C-C-CALM D-D-D-DOWN, EVERYONE!
YOU'RE THE ONE THAT NEEDS TO CALM DOWN!
I-I CAN'T HELP IT...
THUMP
AH...
UM...
I REMEMBER HEARING THAT EIKO-SAN USUALLY ACCOMPANIES THE CHORUS...
BUZZ BUZZ
THUMP
EH?
...TH-THAT'S RIGHT!
EIKO, CAN YOU PLAY?!
GRAB
...EH?
...UM...
THAT'S RIGHT! WE'VE GOT EIKO...
Y-YEAH! I KNOW YOU CAN DO IT!!
BUZZ
AH!
EIKO!
B-BUT...
...I'M SORRY.
BUT PLEASE, EIKO-SAN?
OH...

...OKAY...
I'LL DO MY BEST.
... ALL RIGHT!
THANK YOU.
EIKO, WE'RE COUNTING ON YOU.
WE HARDLY HAVE ANY TIME, BUT LET'S ALL CALM DOWN AND GIVE IT OUR BEST SHOT!
S-SURE.
BUZZ
BUZZ
BUZZ
MUTTER MUTTER
FIVE MINUTES BEFORE SHOWTIME.
BUZZ
TAKAMI-SAN!
BUZZ
AKIRA-KUN ♡
BUZZ
BUZZ
....

TH-THERE ARE SO MANY PEOPLE...
ULP ...
HEY, YOU GUYS! LINE UP!
OKAY, OKAY ...
BUZZ
BUZZ
....
...I GUMMED UP THE WORKS BY DOING THIS...
YAMADA-SAN, MOVE A LITTLE TO THE RIGHT.
... BUT ...
...THE CHORUS SOUNDS WONDERFUL ...
...AND I'M SURE EIKO-SAN'S PIANO...
...WILL BE...
TWEE
THANK YOU FOR YOUR PA-TIENCE.
AND NOW, THE TENTH ANNUAL JOHOKU HIGH CHORUS CLUB CONCERT WILL BEGIN.
KYAAA

AAAA
KYA
TAK
WHERE'S TAKAMI-SAN?
DUE TO AN ACCIDENT, WE'VE MADE A CHANGE IN PIANISTS.
I DEEPLY APOLOGIZE TO THOSE OF YOU WHO WERE LOOKING FORWARD TO HEARING TAKAMI-SAN PLAY.
WHAAAT?!
BEFORE THE PERFORMANCE, THOUGH, I'VE GOT AN ANNOUNCEMENT.
AKIRA-KUN!
CLAP CLAP CLAP CLAP
KYAAA
...HUH?

HOW-EVER...
WE IN THE CHORUS CLUB HAVE PUT OUR HEARTS AND SOULS INTO PREPARING FOR TODAY'S CONCERT...
...SO I HOPE THAT YOU'LL WATCH AND LISTEN TO US THROUGH TO THE END.
BUZZ
I WONDER WHAT HAP-PENED TO TAKAMI-SAN...
I KNOW...
BUZZ
BUZZ
...YIKES...
BUZZ
BUZZ
THEY'RE NOT QUIETING DOWN...
WHAT SHOULD WE...
PLEASE ENJOY.
IT'LL BE ALL RIGHT.
"JOYFUL, JOYFUL."

UWAAA...
THIS IS...

...A LOT BETTER THAN I IMAGINED IT WOULD BE.
WAAAAAA
CLAP CLAP CLAP CLAP CLAP CLAP
WELL...
....
YOU DREW A BIG CROWD...
...AND I ENJOYED YOUR SINGING.
GULP
...OKAY.
VICE PRINCIPAL
PRINCIPAL
I HOPE YOU DO AS GOOD A JOB NEXT YEAR.

THE ONLY STIPULATION IS THAT NEXT TIME, YOU WON'T BE ALLOWED TO USE "OUTSIDE HELP."
WAAAAA
YESSSS!!
OKAY!!
FWISH
YEAH!
GASP
SWISH
C-CLOSE ONE...
......
...TAKAMI-SAN.
DID YOU...
EH?
AH!
...DO ME A FAVOR...
...AND KEEP IT A SECRET?
Ahaha
I'M SO HAPPY FOR YOU GUYS!
ME TOO...

...ALL RIGHT.
CONGRATULATIONS, EVERYBODY!
GREAT JOB!
BUZZ
WELL, HABARA-SAN, SASAKI-KUN...
THE "WRAP PARTY'S" GONNA BE AT A YAKINIKU RESTAURANT AT FOUR.
BUZZ
You can leave the rest of the chairs there.
GREAT.
WE'LL BE THERE.
SEE YOU GUYS LATER!
BUZZ
BUZZ
...
Ahahaha
Really?
Whoop!
... TAKAMI?
AH!
OH! Y-YEAH! YOU READY TO GO?
MICHI-NARI-SAN, I'LL LOCK UP.
EH? YOU SURE?
UH-HUH.
?
WAAA. THEN I'LL LEAVE IT TO YOU!
HEY, AKIRA, EVERYONE'S GONE.
LOCK UP AND LET'S GET GOING.

AH!
EEEEYOWWW!
OUCH!
OWWW!!
...I FIGURED AS MUCH...
FALLING AND SPRAINING YOUR WRIST ON THE DAY OF A PERFORMANCE?
NOT EVEN YOU'RE THAT CLUMSY, TAKAMI.
Heh-heh
....
POKE
HUH?
POKE
...WHAT?
POKE
POKE
POKE
...WHAT'RE YOU POKING ME FOR?
SQUEEZE
WHAT'S YOUR PROB...
GASP
...HEY.
LET ME HEAR YOU PLAY, TAKAMI.
ER, WHAT?
...THE AUDIENCE IS GONE, BUT...
...NO?

...
Y'KNOW...
AKIRA...
YEAH, WHY NOT?
ONE OF THESE DAYS...
Hmm-hmm
Da da da
YANK
THAT'S CUTE.
CRASH
H...
HAH?!
...WHAT ARE YOU DOING? HERE.
I-IT'S YOUR FAULT...
...FOR SAYING WEIRD CRAP!
SLAP

H--

HEY!
WUH...
WHAT DO YOU THINK YOU'RE DOING?!
WHAT IS THIS?!
...AFTER ALL...
...WHY SHOULD MICHINARI-SAN GET TO HAVE ALL THE FUN WITH YOU...? *THAT'S NOT FAIR...*
N-NOT FAIR...?
WHAT ARE YOU, A LITTLE KID...?!
YOU'RE SO KIND, TAKAMI.

THAT'S ONE OF THE THINGS I LOVE ABOUT YOU...
That's changing the subject...
....
SQUEEZE
...WELL... THANKS...
HA HA! YOU'RE RED AS A BEET!
...JACKASS...

カプリチオ
ヴィーナス綺想曲
Phrase.13
VENUS CAPRICCIO

301
HABARA
....
THUMP
THUMP
THUMP
SIGHHH...
....
THUMP
THUMP
... ALL RIGHT.
PUSH
DING

DING
YOU'VE GOTTA BE QUICKER ON THE DRAW, AKIRA.
WHAT WERE YOU HESITATING FOR?
THIS IS...
FWAP
OWWW!
...KIND OF SUDDEN.
HUH! IS THIS THE FIRST TIME AKIRA'S BEEN OVER? THIS IS A SURPRISE...
DAIKI 4TH OLDEST BROTHER (3RD-YEAR HIGH SCHOOL STUDENT)
TANGERINE
APPLE
YEAH, RIGHT? I FIGURED, Y'KNOW, I'M ALWAYS GOING OVER TO HIS HOUSE...
TAKAMI ONLY DAUGHTER (2ND-YEAR HIGH SCHOOL STUDENT)
HERE'S THE MEAT.
SHIN 3RD-OLDEST BROTHER (COLLEGE STUDENT)
I'm not gonna be the one to cook it, though...
KOBE BEEF HIGHEST GRADE
...BUT WE'RE HAVING...
...A YAKINIKU PARTY AT MY PLACE.
BUZZ
BUZZ
I'LL COOK IT!
MEAT
WAIT! THE VEG-ETABLES GO ON FIRST!
THIS ISN'T STEW!

ACTUALLY ...
...THE REASON I CALLED EVERYBODY OVER FOR A PARTY...
...IS BECAUSE YESTERDAY, I WON THE GRAND PRIZE IN A DEPARTMENT STORE DRAWING, A TON OF GRADE-A MEAT.
WE HAVE THE FIRST-PRIZE WINNER OF OUR HIGHEST GRADE JAPANESE BEEF!!
CLANG CLANG
OHHHH!
OH MY!!
I'M HONORED THAT YOU THOUGHT TO INVITE ME...
BUT OF COURSE!
EAT AS MUCH AS YOU LIKE. ♡
SIZZLE
HEY!
I WILL.
HEE-HEE WHAT A HANDSOME MAN. ♡
UM...
ARE YOU SURE IT'S OKAY...
...FOR ME TO BE HERE...?
I MEAN, I DON'T WANT TO BE IN THE WAY...
WHAT ARE YOU TALKING ABOUT, AKIRA?!
HERE, EAT!
THAT'S RIGHT. WE'VE GOT A GREAT BIG BOXFUL OF BEEF, SO STUFF YOURSELF ♡
MM-PH!
I WANT TO PUT TAKAMI'S DRESS ON HIM...
RINNNNNG

RINNNG
RINNNG
MOM, PHONE!
BE RIGHT THERE!
BEEP
YES? HONEY?
SORRY, KYOKO, BUT THERE ARE DOCUMENTS ON TOP OF MY DESK.
COULD YOU BRING THEM HERE?
TAKA-MI-
MMPH
EH? TO YOUR OFFICE?
YEAH.
I DON'T SUPPOSE I HAVE A CHOICE...
WORKING OVERTIME
SORRY ABOUT THIS.
DOCU-MENTS AGAIN?
THAT'S RIGHT.
WHAT CAN I DO? I'LL BE BACK AS SOON AS I CAN.
ODA-SENSEI, YOU'RE IN CHARGE.
ALL RIGHT. BE CAREFUL.
I'M REALLY SORRY ABOUT THIS...
AH! IT'LL TAKE ME OVER TWO HOURS TO GET THERE AND BACK...
...BUT MINORS, NO DRINKING!!
BUMP
UMPH!
MOM
WHOOPS.

RIKUTO 2ND-OLDEST BROTHER (22)
SORRY, MA!
HEY, THE GANG'S ALL HERE...
Haven't been home in a while
KEEP IT DOWN!
...AH!
AKIRA!!
OUCH... ...I FORGOT YOU WERE COMING, RIKUTO.
WHERE'S SHU?
HE SAID HE COULDN'T MAKE IT BECAUSE OF WORK.
TOO BAD
SHU, OLDEST BROTHER (24)
AH... THANK YOU FOR LETTING ME INTO YOUR H--
...OME.
THANKS FOR COMING, MAN! GOD, YOU'VE GOTTEN BIG! I HAVEN'T TALKED TO YOU SINCE THAT ONE TIME*!!
WHAT HAPPENED TO YOU AFTER THAT, DUDE? I'M ALWAYS SURPRISED WHEN I HEAR YOU AND TAKAMI HAVE STUCK TOGETHER ALL THESE YEARS!
I MEAN, HOW CAN YOU STAND HER?
GRAB
I CAN HEAR YOU, BUTTHEAD!
* SEVERAL YEARS AGO, AKIRA WENT OUT FOR CAKE WITH TAKAMI AND HER FAMILY AFTER PARTICIPATING IN A PIANO COMPETITION.

GIVE IT TO ME STRAIGHT! WHAT'S THE SITCH BETWEEN YOU TWO? ♡
WHAT? HE'S JUST ASKING A QUESTION.
RIGHT, AKIRA?
AH...
...UMM...
SNATCH
YOU'RE BOTHERING HIM!!
KILL-JOY!
HMPH.
Jeez!
REALLY SORRY ABOUT THEM. HERE, GET BACK IN THE MOOD BY EATING MORE...
CRAP... HE'S OVER-WHELMED BY MY BROTHERS...
L-LET'S HAVE SOME MORE MEAT.
AH... YEAH.
GASP
PLUS, I DON'T THINK HE'S COMFORTABLE IN A NOISY ENVIRONMENT LIKE THIS...
I INVITED AKIRA, THINKING THAT IF HE'S WITH ME...
...I'LL BE SURE TO HAVE A GREAT TIME, BUT...
...MAYBE I SHOULD HAVE THOUGHT TWICE.
WHAM
ALL RIGHT. SEEING AS WE GOT SO MANY PEOPLE HERE...
...LET'S PLAY THE KING GAME!

...FORGET IT.
I'LL PLAY!
THAT'S THE SPIRIT, SHINOBU-SAN!
ALTHOUGH TAKAMI BEING THE ONLY FEMALE HERE TAKES SOME OF THE FUN OUT OF IT!
WHAP
WHAT GAME IS IT? IT SOUNDS LIKE FUN...
NEVER MIND, AKIRA. RIKU IS A SADIST WHEN IT COMES TO THAT GAME.
THEN I'LL PLAY A WOMAN FOR THE GAME...
YEAH, PLEASE DON'T.
YAYYY
FWIP
YOU GUYS DO WHAT YOU WANT. NO WAY AM I GONNA PLAY.
SEEMS TO HAVE SUFFERED HORRIBLY WHILE PLAYING THE GAME IN THE PAST
ME NEITHER.
AH! HEY, IS ALL THE GINGER ALE GONE?
YOU CAN HAVE MINE. I BARELY TOUCHED IT.
EMPTY
SKRITCH
SKRITCH
MM? OH, THIS CUP.
WHAT KIND OF GAME IS IT?
GULP
GULP
IT'S REALLY FUN!

ONE MINUTE LATER
DRAW.
DUN
...LOOK...
IF YOU THINK YOU HAVE THE POWER TO MAKE EVERYONE OBEY YOU...
...YOU'RE SORELY MISTAKEN.

RUMBLE
RUMBLE
DID YOU SAY SOME-THING ...?
RUMBLE
Ulp ...
I'LL DRAW ONE NOW...

Yay! I'm number three!
HAPPY AS LONG AS THINGS ARE FUN
3
There is a god!
GRAB
KIN
I...
...I DID IT...
I...
KING
UNHHHHHHH
I'M THE KING!

HUH? MY BEER'S GONE.
RIKUTO-KUN, DID YOU DRINK...
TODAY...
HIC
...'CAUSE IT'S...
FWISH
AH!
...YOU DO WHAT I SAY...
WOBBLE
EVERY-ONE...
...MY MEAT!

2

ABOUT COLORS.

MY EDITOR LET ME DO COLOR ILLUSTRATIONS (SEE VOLUME ONE).

THE COLOR INK I USE IS DR. MARTIN AND NOUVELLE, BUT I NOTICED THAT I'VE HARDLY BEEN USING THE INK THAT I PURCHASED AFTER THAT FIRST ILLUSTRATION.

WHAT A WASTE...

FROM HERE ON OUT, I WANNA TRY EXPERIMENTING WITH DIFFERENT COLORS.

AFTER I'M DONE COLORING THE ART, I LOVE SPRAY PAINTING THE BORDER.

AH,
I ALSO USE COPIC INK.
THAT'S EXTREMELY CONVENIENT.
AND I USE COLORED PENCILS AND SOMETIMES PASTELS, TOO.

(THE END)

SORRY TO KEEP YOU WAITING ♡
ORDER: FOR NUMBERS 1 AND 3 TO DRESS IN WOMAN'S CLOTHING
......
AGAINST HIS WILL
Gyaha-haha! This is a riot!
#1 (DAIKI)
#3 (SHINOBU)
TAKAMI'S DRESS
Ahahaha-haha
DAIKI, YOU'RE ADORABLE. SHINOBU-SAN, YOU'RE GORGEOUS!! YOU'VE GOT BEAUTIFUL LEGS! AHAHA! ♡
GYAHA-HAHA!
A-AKIRA...?
I-I THOUGHT YOU, OF ALL PEOPLE, WOULD UNDERSTAND HOW I FEEL...
MOM'S WIG
MOM'S BLOUSE
TAKAMI'S SHORTS
...I'M SORRY... I CAN'T...
PFFF!
ET TU, AKIRA...?!?
GONG
SH-SHINOBU-SAN...
DIDN'T MY MOM PUT YOU IN CHARGE?! WHAT ARE YOU DOING PLAYING THE GAME...?!
ACTUALLY A PERSON WITH COMMON SENSE.
Of course, I'll have to apologize to your mother that Takami drank alcohol...
I THOUGHT AS LONG AS IT WAS FUN, WHY NOT?
I'M NOT HAVING ANY FUN! THIS IS MORTIFYING!

I'M NOT DONE WITH YOU GUYS YET!
SHIN-CHAN, FEED ME!!
AREN'T YOU EVEN GONNA CALL A NUMBER?!
IF I MUST...
DELI-CIOUS!
I'M GLAD.
AKIRA, GIVE DAIKI A MASSAGE!!
?! TO ME?!
OKAY.
My turn?! THUMP THUMP
S-SORRY ABOUT THIS!
REALLY. I MEAN, YOUR FIRST TIME HERE AND YOU GET SHANGHAIED INTO THIS...
SHOULDER RUB
THAT'S ALL RIGHT. IT'S FUN.
RIKU, PUT SHINOBU-SAN IN A SLEEPER HOLD!!
EH?!
GOTCHA!!
EH?
WAIT!
YOU'RE NOT REALLY...
WAHA-HAHAHA
I give up!
I give up!
Wa-haha-haha

I give up!
WAHA-HAHAHA
...WILL SOMEBODY PLEASE STOP HER...?
HEY!
TAKAMI-CHAN, YOU'RE GONNA CATCH COLD SLEEPING ON THE FLOOR LIKE THAT.
P-PLEASE DON'T WAKE HER UP... SHE FINALLY WENT TO SLEEP...
CRUNCH CRUNCH
Zzzz Zzzz
SLUMP
Zzzzz
DAIKI-SAN...
HERE. I RAN IT UNDER THE FAUCET.
EH? AH! SORRY.
LIPSTICK SMEARED ON BY TAKAMI
IT'S OKAY.

MAYBE IT'S TIME TO START CLEANING UP...
I'LL TAKE THE DISHES TO THE KITCHEN.
YOU'RE A GREAT GUY.
OH! I KNEW YOU'D STEP UP, AKIRA-KUN.
IGNORE
You're cold!
LEAVING IT TO OTHER PEOPLE
TAKAMI... CAN YOU DRINK SOME WATER?
LATER...
...'M SLEEP-PY...
ALL RIGHT.

MMM...
I'M GOING TO PUT...
... TAKAMI TO BED.
AH... YEAH, OKAY.
AH! WHICH ONE IS TAKAMI'S ROOM?
AT THE END OF THE HALL.
OKAY.
GOT IT.
UH...
HE'S IN JUNIOR HIGH...?
Scary, I know...
THAT'S RIGHT. YOU'D NEVER THINK...
THAT'S HILARIOUS!
Wahaha!

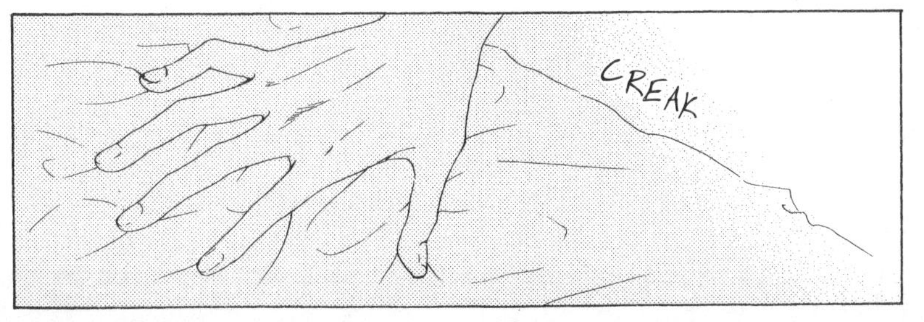
CREAK

...SORRY, TAKAMI.
I'VE GOT YOU IN BACKWARDS.
MMM...
RUSTLE
ZZZZZZZ
GOOD NI--
...LAST...
...ORDER...
GRAB
?!
AKIRA...

PLAY ME... ...A LULLABY ...
SQUEEZE
......
HEH.
...AS YOU COM-MAND.
HEY.
THAT SOUNDS NICE...
THAT'S AKIRA, ISN'T IT?
TAKAMI COULD NEVER PRODUCE A GENTLE SOUND LIKE THAT... ...AH... I'VE HEARD THIS BEFORE... WHERE WAS IT...?
TAN-GERINE
IT'S FOSTER'S "BEAUTIFUL DREAMER." YOU HEAR IT A LOT WHEN YOU'RE ON THE PHONE AND SOMEBODY PUTS YOU ON HOLD.

YEAH, THAT'S RIGHT. *HUH...*
IT SOUNDS WAY DIFFERENT ON THE PIANO...
HIC
...THANK YOU.

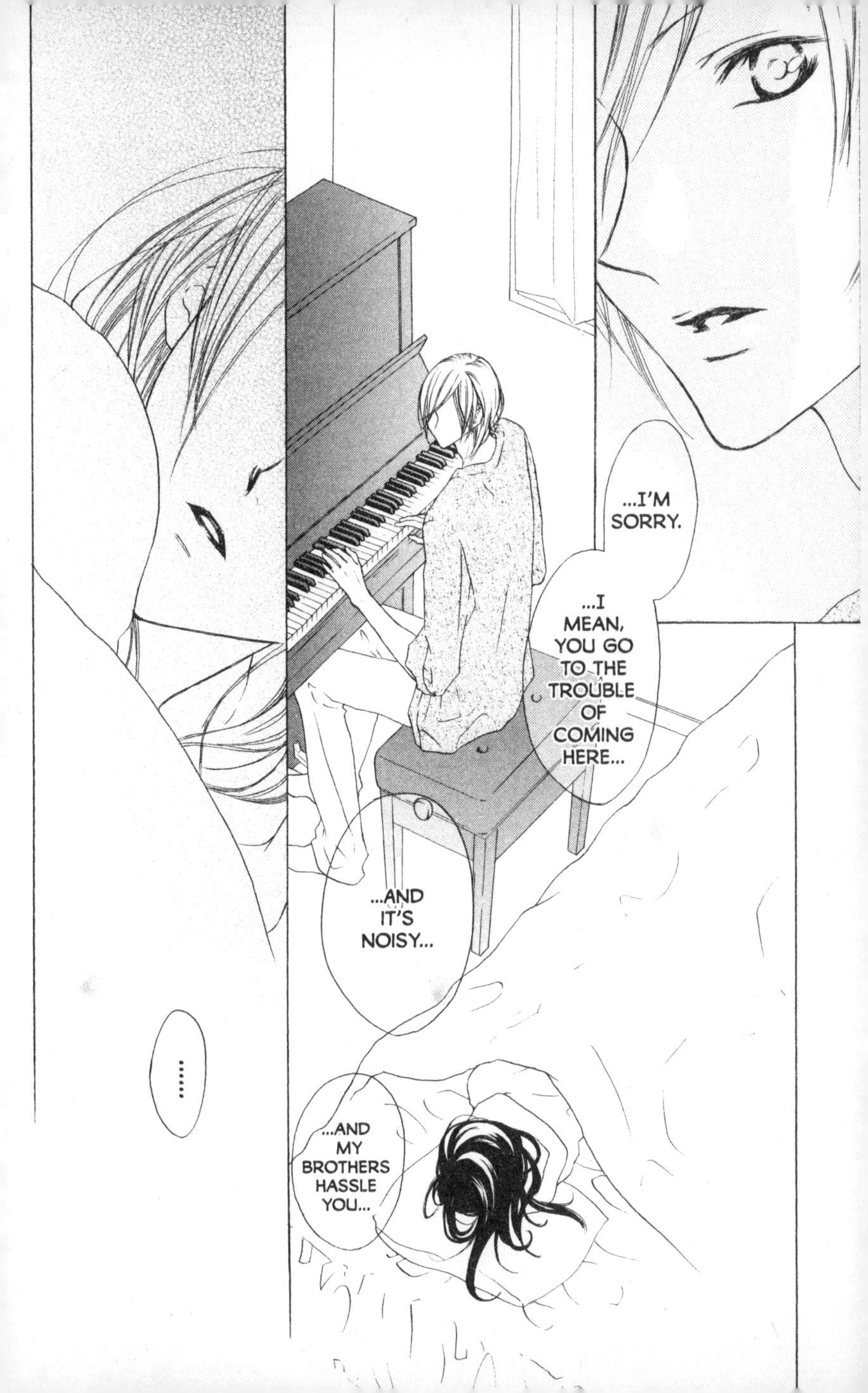

...I'M SORRY.
...I MEAN, YOU GO TO THE TROUBLE OF COMING HERE...
...AND IT'S NOISY...
...AND MY BROTHERS HASSLE YOU...
......

BUT STILL...
THANK YOU...
...FOR COMING.
ZZZZ...
SMACK SMACK
THANK *YOU.*

TAK
I HAD FUN...
...SPENDING TIME WITH YOU...
...AND ALL OF THE WARM PEOPLE AROUND YOU.
RUSTLE
AKIRA... AKI...

CREAK

FEELS LIKE A CRIMINAL
Z z z z
....
G--
GOOD-NIGHT...
TAKAMI ...
MMM ...
TAK TAK
RUSTLE
AH!

AKIRA...
I REALLY GOTTA APOLOGIZE TO YOU, MAN! YOU SHOULDN'T HAVE HAD TO BE PUT THROUGH THAT...
NO, IT'S OKAY....
I HAD FUN.
COME ON, THERE'S NO REASON FOR YOU TO HOLD BACK! I MEAN, EVEN THE ADULTS HERE ACT AS IRRESPONSIBLY AS KIDS...
LAID-BACK
WE ARE.
LIAR!
HEY, ADULTS!! BE GRATEFUL HE'S GOING EASY ON YOU!
...NO, REALLY.
...THIS WAS MY FIRST TIME HERE...
...SO I WAS NERVOUS, BUT...
...UM, I'M AN ONLY CHILD...
...SO BEING HERE...
... MADE ME FEEL WHAT IT MIGHT BE LIKE TO HAVE BROTHERS.
I HAD A GREAT TIME.

TH--
THIS IS THE KIND OF LITTLE SISTER I WANTED...
I-I SEE. IN THAT CASE, I'M GLAD...
...HUH? AKIRA, IS YOUR FACE RED? WHAT'S WRONG?
HUH?
DID YOU...
...GIVE HER A KISS OR SOME-THING?
TAKAMI'S ROOM
DAZ
ED
WHAT?

SERI-OUSLY?!
YOU DID?! YOU KISSED HER?! KYAAA!! ♡♡
NO... UM, I-I...
HMPH. SO YOU TWO ARE LIKE THAT?
KYAAAA!!

AH... NO. I THINK OF HER THAT WAY, BUT SHE DOESN'T...
Kyaaa
HUH.
AH. S...
SORRY. I SHOULDN'T HAVE SAID...
DON'T DO IT, MAN!

YOU CAN FIND A MUCH BETTER WOMAN, AKIRA!!
BROADEN YOUR HORIZONS WHILE YOU'RE STILL YOUNG!
DID YOU KNOW THAT WHEN SHE FLIES OFF THE HANDLE, SHE'LL PUT YOU IN A PRO WRESTLING HOLD?!
SHE'S BOW-LEGGED AND HAS A NASTY MOUTH!
NOT ONLY THAT...
YOU'RE IN FOR IT...
Heh-heh
Too late?
.... GROAN
GRIN GRIN

カプリチオ
ヴィーナス綺想曲
Phrase.14
VENUS
CaPRICCIO

DING-DONG
DING-DONG
MEISHIN JUNIOR HIGH SCHOOL
KEI.
YOU KNOW ABOUT THE ARCADE THAT JUST OPENED BY THE STATION?
3-A
Bye-bye!
See you later!
DON'T GOT ANY MONEY.
TAK
TAK
YOU NEVER DO.
WHAT DO YA WANT ME TO DO, MAN?
FOO
THEY GOT POOL TABLES, TOO.
HMPH.

TAK
AKIRA-KUN, BYE-BYE!
GRIN
HE SMILED!
AHHHH... I WISH I COULD WALK HOME WITH HIM!
COME TO THINK OF IT, AKIRA-KUN ALWAYS LEAVES BY HIMSELF.
IN FACT, HE'S USUALLY ALONE. LIKE A PRINCE WHO HOLDS HIMSELF APART FROM THE CROWD.
I KNOW. ♡
GASP
D-DON'T LOOK AT US, AZEGAMI!
WE'D NEVER WALK HOME WITH YOU...
I'M NOT LOOKING AT YOU!
Gross...
Meishin's problem child!! The difference between you and Akira-kun is the difference between night and day!
YEAH, YEAH, WHATEVER. LET'S GO.
Gyaaa!
TAK TAK
WHAT ABOUT THE ARCADE?
EVERY FRIDAY...
...AFTER SCHOOL IS "PIANO TIME."
駅

S 駅
TAKAMI!
AKIRA AND I MEET UP HERE..
HEY!
...THEN HEAD OVER TO THE PIANO SCHOOL.
ON THE WAY HOME, LET'S GET SOMETHING TO EAT.
YOU'RE TALKING ABOUT "THE WAY HOME" ALREADY ...?
WHAT? YOU DON'T WANNA?
NO, WE CAN, BUT...
THEN IT'S SET. ♡
S 駅
THIS RITUAL AT THE BEGINNING OF THE WEEKEND...
...HASN'T CHANGED SINCE WE FIRST MET.
BUT THIS DAY...

SASAKI.
YO.
...WOULD PROVE TO BE A LITTLE DIFFERENT.
HUH...
I WAS WONDERING WHERE YOU WERE GOIN'...
MM?
AKIRA, ARE THESE YOUR FRIENDS?
... CLASSMATES.
I WOULDN'T CONSIDER THEM FRIENDS.
Y'KNOW, SASAKI, I HAD YOU PEGGED AS A LONELY SAD SACK WITHOUT ANY FRIENDS.
BUT GUESS I WAS WRONG, HUH? NOT BAD. THIS YOUR WOMAN?
FOO
UWAAA! WHAT THE HELL?!
GET YOUR PAW OFF...
GRAB

...YOU WERE "WONDERING WHERE I WAS GOING"...?
AZEGAMI ...
WERE YOU...
...FOLLOWING ME?
SLARE
AH!
OF COURSE NOT, DUMMY!! WHY THE HECK WOULD I...
THERE! I WAS ON MY WAY TO THAT ARCADE!!
THERE
BREAK·S
CAFE·GAME
BILLIARDS
NEW OPEN
THAT HURT.
THAT WAS THE POINT! AND I CAN MAKE IT A LOT WORSE!
FLICK
FLICK
HEY ...
OUCH!
MM?
Azegami...
......

IF YOU'RE REALLY A MAN, YOU'D AT LEAST GO TO THE ARCADE WITH US, 'STEADA PLAYIN' THAT PIANO ALL THE TIME!
...NO THANKS.
TWITCH
UWAAA! THEN HE IS A GIRL!!
WIMP! LITTLE GIRL!
MEMORY OF THEIR CHILDHOOD * SEE VOLUME 1
GYAAA GYAAA
TWITCH
AH!!
YOU!!
WHA...?
Y...
...YOU...
SWISH
DON'T BULLY AKIRA!
DUMMY! STUPID KEI!!
STUPID KEI...

AH! YOU. TAKAMI, RIGHT?
I didn't recognize you.
PFF
What? Who is she?
THE ONLY THING DIFFERENT ABOUT YOU IS THAT YOU GREW YOUR HAIR OUT.
W-WHY, YOU...
THE ONLY THING DIFFERENT ABOUT YOU IS YOU'RE A BEANPOLE NOW!
TAKAMI, LET'S GO.
What, I shoulda changed more?!
HUH. SO NOW YOU'RE ABLE TO STEP UP A LITTLE AND PROTECT AN OLDER GIRL...
...AKIRA-CHAN?
A MORON LIKE YOU DOESN'T HAVE THE RIGHT TO USE "CHAN" WITH AKIRA'S NAME!
TAKAMI, COME ON.
LET IT GO.
BUT HE...
I'VE GOT AN IDEA.
WE WERE JUST GONNA SHOOT SOME POOL.
Come on, who is she?
WHY DON'T YOU TWO JOIN US?
YEAH, RIGHT! YOU'RE CLUELESS IF YOU THINK WE'D WASTE TIME ON YOU!
TA TA TA
STUPID KEI!
...HEY, SASAKI.

RATHER THAN HANG OUT WITH HER ALL THE TIME...
...YOU OUGHTA CHILL WITH DUDES FROM SCHOOL ONCE IN A WHILE.
Sigh...
IT'S NOT LIKE I'M GOING ON A DATE.
NYAAAAAH
WE'RE GOING TO PIANO SCHOOL! REMEMBER?! THE ONE YOU QUIT!
KEI, YOU PLAYED THE PIANO?
Go figure...
I CAN'T PICTURE IT.
LET'S PLAY POOL.
FWAP
....
...... YOU GOT FINGERPRINTS ON MY GLASSES...

NOW THAT HE MENTIONS IT...
"I HAD YOU PEGGED AS A LONELY SAD SACK WITHOUT ANY FRIENDS."
FOOO...
...I'VE NEVER SEEN AKIRA WITH ANY FRIENDS FROM SCHOOL.
"RATHER THAN HANG OUT WITH HER ALL THE TIME..."
...
"...YOU OUGHTA CHILL WITH DUDES FROM SCHOOL ONCE IN A WHILE."
I WONDER ...
IF AKIRA...
...HAS ANY FRIENDS...?
THE FOLLOWING WEEK (FRIDAY).
AOYAMA PIANO SCHOOL

3

I WANT TO TRY COLORING WITH A COMPUTER.

MY PROBLEM, THOUGH, IS THAT I ALWAYS SAY I ***WANT*** TO DO SOMETHING, BUT IT DOESN'T TRANSLATE INTO ACTION.

I DID GET A TABLET AND COLORING SOFTWARE. SO I DREW A PICTURE, UPLOADED IT INTO THE TABLET, MESSED AROUND WITH IT A BIT AND WAS SATISFIED. BUT THEN I SET IT ASIDE AND DIDN'T FINISH IT.

SIGH...

BUT I REALLY WANNA DO IT! (I WANT TO FINISH COLORING THE PICTURE.) I'VE GOT THE ENTHUSIASM FOR IT.

I'LL DO IT... SOMETIME!

YES, I WILL FINISH COLORING THAT ART!!

...WHERE IS HE?
"HE?"
...SASAKI.
...
AKIRA?
HE WAS A LITTLE LATE GETTING ON THE TRAIN, SO I'LL MEET HIM AT THE SCHOOL.
...OH.
WELL, SEE YA.
HUH?
YEAH...
TAK TAK TAK
SEE YA...
...WHAT WAS THAT?
"I WAS JUST WALKIN' BY."
JUST WALKING BY...
S STATION
ARCADE
S STREET
MAIN STREET
HERE
AOYAMA PIANO SCHOOL
DEAD END
......
MY EYE, HE WAS.

"WERE YOU FOLLOWING ME?"
"WE WERE JUST GONNA SHOOT SOME POOL. WHY DON'T YOU TWO JOIN US?"
"I HAD YOU PEGGED AS A LONELY SAD SACK WITHOUT ANY FRIENDS."
FRIEND...
FLASH
AH!
CLAMP
DOES THIS GUY...
...WANT TO...?
HUH?
NOW WHAT...?
HEY, YOU MENTIONED POOL.
WHUH?
THE DAY AFTER TOMORROW.
SUNDAY.
LET'S SHOOT SOME POOL!

...HAH?
YOU'RE THE ONE THAT SHOT ME DOWN BEFORE.
I LOVE POOL!
MY BIG BROTHER SHU'S THE ONLY ONE I CAN'T BEAT.
THAT NEW PLACE ON S STREET IS GOOD, YEAH?
HEY...
THEN IT'S SETTLED! SUNDAY AFTER LUNCH. WE'LL MEET THERE!!
WHY ME...?
I'LL INVITE AKIRA, TOO.
CREAK
HMPH...
....

AND SO...
SUNDAY
TAKAMI...
BREAK · S
CAFE · GAME
BILLIARDS

WHAT IS THIS?
...HEY.

DON'T POINT!
...
SQUEAK SQUEAK
KEI PRACTICALLY BEGGED ME TO PLAY...
SO COME ON. A COUPLE GAMES WON'T HURT.
?! WHAT?!
I DIDN'T SAY ANYTHING LIKE THAT! YOU TOLD ME TO COME HERE...
...BEGGED YOU TO PLAY? I DON'T UNDERSTAND.
AZEGAMI, DO YOU HAVE A THING FOR TAKAMI...?
WHAT?! LIKE I'D FALL FOR "BUTCH" HERE?! AS IF!!
SNAP CRACKLE
OH, FOR PETE'S SAKE! I DON'T NEED THIS! I'M GOIN' HOME!!
SO YOU'RE GONNA RUN AWAY?
FWAP
FREEZE
RUMBLE RUMBLE RUMBLE RUMBLE
CRACKLE CRACKLE CRACKLE CRACKLE CRACKLE

YOU'RE ACCUSING THE GUY KNOWN AS "THE HUS-TLER OF MEISHIN JUNIOR HIGH" OF RUNNING AWAY...?
RUMBLE RUMBLE RUMBLE RUMBLE RUMBLE
I'VE NEVER PLAYED BEFORE, SO I DON'T CARE.
I haven't heard that about you.
I thought I was just gonna have lunch with Takami today.
WHUNK

TAKAMI VS. KEI 9 BALL SHOWDOWN
I WIN!
HA HA
....
I don't believe it...
HEH.
"HEH"?
DON'T GIVE ME "HEH"! A MENTAL SPORT LIKE BILLIARDS, AND I LOSE TO THIS BROAD?!
THIS PISSES ME OFF TO NO END!!
HA-HA-HA-HA-HA-HA
HUH.
DON'T GIVE ME "HUH" EITHER, JACK-ASS!
Heh-heh
NOW YOU PLAY AGAINST ME, AKIRA.
THE RULES ARE SIMPLE.

WHUNK

WA HA HA HA HA HA HA!
WEAK!
...
Of course! This is his first time...
...
YOU...
...AND YOU...
Huh?
HA HA HA HA HA
...ARE WEAK!!
Wench...
......
CERTAINLY...
...IT'S FRUS-TRATING, ISN'T IT?
...ISN'T THAT WHAT I SAID...?
ALL RIGHT.

I'LL GIVE YOU A HANDICAP.
I'LL PLAY AGAINST BOTH OF YOU.
Heh-heh
WELL?
......
BOTH OF US...?
...WELL, I SUPPOSE...
YOU'RE GONNA REGRET THIS, TAKAMI.
...HEH.
WHUNK

WAHAHAHA! THAT'S ONE GAME FOR ME!
HRRR...
Too easy...
GAME TWO.
AH!
SLIP
SASAKI...
AND SO...
TWO VICTORIES FOR TAKAMI
CRAP...
YAYYY!
WAHOO!
GIRL'S A SHARK...
THREE WINS FOR TAKAMI
Damn, she's tough...
HUFF HUFF
NOOOO! JEEZ!
LIKE THIS! THIS!! RELAX YOUR SHOULDERS, SASAKI!
YOU'RE TOO TENSE!
L-LIKE THIS?
YES! AND SHOOT LIKE THIS!
Ah! YOUR ELBOW'S WEIRD.
JERK
THAT HURTS... A LITTLE.
JUST TRY TO DO WHAT I SAY!
HEH.
WHUNK
OH!

YOU KNOCKED IT IN. *YOUR FIRST POCKET.*
UH-HUH.
YOU'VE BOTH STILL GOT A LONG WAY TO GO.
CAN I TAKE...
...ONE MORE TURN?
...HUH?
YEAH. GO AHEAD. *KNOCK ANOTHER ONE IN.*
TAK
KLAK
WHUNK
OH!
DUDE, YOU'RE GETTING THE HANG OF IT.
...YEAH.
...IT'S FEELS LIKE...
FOO

...I'M GETTING A BETTER GRASP OF THE GAME AS WE GO.
WHUNK
WOW...
EASY, ACE.
LET YOUR PARTNER HAVE A CHANCE TO LOOK COOL.

WHUNK
OH!
WH
YIKES!
UNK
KEI'S BALL
AKIRA'S BALL
I GOTTA ADMIT, I DIDN'T SEE THIS COMIN'.
HEH-HEH.
...ONE MORE BALL TO GO...
...ALL RIGHT. LEAVE IT TO ME.
TAK
KZAK
FOOOO
FREEZE
...AH!! HEY!!
GO IN! GET IN THERE!

WHUNK
OH!
YESSS!
SLAP
THAT'S WHAT I'M TALKIN' ABOUT!
YA SEE THAT, TAKA...
GASP

FWISH
...ANY WAY...
I...
HMPH
I KNOCKED MOST OF THE BALLS IN.
YEAH, WHATEVER.
......
Rrrrr...
...Y'KNOW, THAT'S JUST LIKE YOU.
YOU BREEZE THROUGH EVERY-THING WITH THAT NONCHA-LANT FACE.
QUIT IN SIXTH GRA-DE
:
BACK THEN
WITH THE PIANO, TOO. ANY PIECE OF MUSIC AN' YOU PLAYED IT WITH NO HESITATION, NO MISTAKES... LIKE IT WAS WRITTEN FOR YOU.
YOU KNOW HOW JEALOUS I WAS OF...
GASP

......
I...
I MEAN ...
HUH... SO YOU WERE JEALOU...
MMMPH
NOTHING! ...I...
I'M GOING HOME!!
TROMP
TROMP
TROMP
TROMP
TROMP
...
...HEY, WAIT.
LET'S PLAY AGAIN SOMETIME, KEI.
HMPH!
WHY THE HECK WOULD I WANNA PLAY AGAIN WITH YOU TW--
TUG
AAAAH!

WHISPER
YOU...
...WANTED TO BECOME AKIRA'S FRIEND, DIDN'T YOU?
BLUSH
FREEZE
....
......
TROMP TROMP
PFFF
SAY WHAT YOU WANT!

NEXT TIME, TEACH ME THE PIANO...
...SASAKI.
BLANK
......
GAH!
I SHOULDN'T'VE SAID ANYTHI--
I DON'T MIND.

I COULD TEACH YOU...
...Y-YEAH?
GASP
AH... I MEAN, UH...
ALL RIGHT!
SEE YA LATER, AKIRA!
TROMP TROMP
WHIRRR
......

WEIRDO...
ON A WEEK END...
...THE SAME AS ANY OTHER...
...I HEARD A SOUND...
...THAT I'D NEVER HEARD BEFORE.
THE NEXT DAY
AOYAMA PIANO SCHOOL
GASP
......
APPLICATION FORM

カプリチオ
ヴィーナス綺想曲
VENUS CAPRICCIO
Phrase.15

カプリチオ
ヴィーナス綺想曲
VENUS
CAPRICCIO

AOYAMA PIANO SCHOOL
AOYAMA PIANO SCHOOL
FLASH
FLASH
FL
ASH
FL
ASH
AHAHAHAHA HAHAHA HAHAHA
CACKLE CACKLE
H-HEY ... COME ON, YOU GUYS...
KYAHA-HAHAHA
LOOK, FELLAS...

HAR, HAR. OKAY, YOU'VE HAD YOUR YUKS.
NOW CAN YOU JUST LET ME TAKE ONE DECENT PICTURE? PRETTY PLEASE?
TH...
THAT'S RIGHT!
YOUR WORDS SAY ONE THING, BUT YOUR FACE TELLS A DIFFERENT STORY!
SHUT UP, TAKAMI!
YEAH, SHUT UP!
A GUY YOUR SIZE SITTIN' LIKE A GIRL IS JUST WRONG!!
B-BOYS, WE DON'T HAVE ALL DAY...
BRATS... ARE YOU ALWAYS THIS RUDE WHEN YOU MEET SOMEONE FOR THE FIRST TIME? I CAN'T HELP THE WAY I SIT.
AHAHAHAHA
SHIVER SHIVER
6'4"
FINE. IF YOU'RE NOT GOING TO BEHAVE, I'LL TAKE IT LIKE THIS.
THIS IS REIICHI TSUCHIYA-SAN, A FREELANCE CAMERAMAN.
(AGE UNKNOWN).
SATISFIED NOW?
FLASH
AHAHAHAHA
PFFAAA!
I CAN'T HOLD IT IN!

EXCUSE ME, AOYAMA-SAN.
YOU NEVER TOLD ME I'D HAVE TO TAKE PHOTOS OF RUGRATS LIKE THESE.
Honestly...
Who you callin' a rugrat?!
NOW, NOW...
HE'S AN ACQUAINTANCE OF AOYAMA-SAN...
...AND IS TAKING PICTURES OF ALL OF US FOR A NEW PAMPHLET ADVERTISING THE SCHOOL.
AOYAMA
ピアノ教室
LET ME HOLD THE CAMERA!
BUZZ
BUZZ
NOT ON YOUR LIFE!
OH!
TO BE HONEST, I'M NOT REALLY COMFORTABLE HAVING MY PICTURE TAKEN...
My smile always comes off forced...
POLAROID TAKEN A FEW MINUTES AGO
HUH? THIS ONE LOOKS NORMAL. WHEN DID HE TAKE THAT...?
...THIS IS THE MOST NATURAL I'VE SEEN MYSELF IN A PHOTOGRAPH... MAYBE IT'D BE GOOD FOR THE PAMPHLET...
I WANT THIS PICTURE...
YOU CAN KEEP THAT IF YOU LIKE.
EH?
R-REALLY?!
B-BUT I THOUGHT YOU MIGHT USE IT FOR THE PAMPHLET...
...BUT GETTING IT TAKEN BY HIM...
...HAS BEEN KIND OF FUN.

...THIS IS MY FIRST TIME SEEING A GAY GUY IN REAL LIFE...
He sounds like a woman.
AS FAR AS YOU KNOW.
THERE MAY BE MORE AROUND THAN YOU REALIZE, POSSIBLY RIGHT UNDER YOUR NOSE...
A LITTLE HOMOPHOBIC, ARE WE?
I'M OVER HERE BECAUSE OF THE CREEPY WAY YOU TOUCHED ME... I DIDN'T KNOW THAT ABOUT YOU, SENSEI.
I WASN'T REFERRING TO MYSELF.
THEN GIVE IT BACK.
WAAA! NO! I WAS KIDDING!
I want it!
CHUCKLE
Sigh...
NOW I JUST NEED TO TAKE SOME PICS OF THE LESSONS...
UM... AOYAMA-SENSEI...
CAN I ASK YOU SOMETHING?
MM? WHAT IS IT, AKIRA-KUN?
THAT'S RIGHT... I HAVEN'T TAKEN ANY SHOTS OF...
...THIS BEAUTIFUL BOY YET.

...SO I'D LIKE TO HAVE THAT SCORE, IF POSSIBLE...
...BUT IT LOOKS LIKE IT'S NOT AVAILABLE IN JAPAN...
HMM... INDEED.
THEN I'LL SEND AWAY FOR IT FROM OVERSEAS...
...
...ALL RIGHT.
THANK YOU.
HUH? NOW THERE'S A CALM BOY.
AKIRA! AKIRA!
HAVE HIM TAKE YOUR PICTURE, TOO!
Oh! THAT'S RIGHT!
COME ON! HE CAN TAKE A PICTURE OF US TOGETHER!
MAYBE IT'D EVEN BE USED IN THE PAMPHLET!!
...NO NEED. HE CAN TAKE MORE PHOTOS OF YOU, TAKA--
SHAKE
SHAKE
...JUST A MINUTE.
Take my picture! Take my picture!

Okay?!
LET'S HAVE ONE TAKEN!
REALLY, I DON'T NEED...
IT'S NOT WHAT YOU NEED! ALL RIGHT?!
AH!
I PROMISE TO BUY YOU A PIECE OF CAKE ON THE WAY HOME!
PFF! WHY WOULD YOU NEED TO TREAT ME?
AH! JERK! DON'T LAUGH AT ME!
AHAHAHAHA
SAY...
...YOU TWO...

4

MY MOM BROUGHT HOME A KITTEN.

I'VE GOT FOUR YOUNGER SISTERS AND TWO OF THEM ARE SOMEWHAT ALLERGIC TO CATS, SO I THINK WE'RE IN FOR SOME DIFFICULTIES AROUND HERE. ALTHOUGH, HAVING SAID THAT, THERE'S ALWAYS BEEN A CAT IN OUR HOUSE. I'M NOT AS ALLERGIC AS MY SISTERS, BUT SOMETIMES, EVEN I CAN'T SPEND A LONG TIME AROUND A KITTEN OR I START SNEEZING AND MY NOSE RUNS. AND THEN THERE ARE OTHER TIMES WHERE I'M FINE NO MATTER HOW LONG I'M BY THEM, SO GO FIGURE.

EITHER WAY...

I LOVE CATS!!

I REALLY LOVE CATS!!

SO MUCH I CAN'T REALLY EXPRESS IT IN WORDS!!

I'M SO THRILLED THAT NOW THERE ARE TWO CATS IN THE HOUSE!!

MODELING FOR YOUR ONE-MAN EXHIBITION?
UH-HUH. IT'S STILL A WAYS OFF, BUT I'M GOING TO EXHIBIT MY PHOTOS.
I MAINLY DO SCENERY, BUT SEEING YOU TWO TOGETHER...
WELL, WELL...
...STIRRED SOMETHING UP INSIDE OF ME.
DUNNNNNN
giggle giggle
OH...
Don't get the wrong idea!
OH, DEAR! I JUST MEANT IN TERMS OF A PHOTOGRAPHIC SUBJECT!
FWAP
KOFF
OKAY! I'LL DO IT! I WANNA DO IT!!
REALLY? THANK YOU!
...WHAT ABOUT YOU, AKIRA-KUN?
...IF TAKAMI'S GOING TO DO IT...
WAIT A SECOND, MR. PHOTOG-RAPHER!!

FOO
FW
ISH
IF IT'S A MODEL THAT YOU WANT...
...OLOOK NO FURTHER.
IMAGINE THE FRESH PHOTOS YOU'D TAKE WITH JUST AKIRA AND ME!
WAIT A SECOND, YOU TWO!
KYAAA. I LOVE IT! I THINK I'LL USE YOU ALL.
BUZZ BUZZ
GYAAA GYAAA
IS IT ALL RIGHT IF I BORROW YOUR STUDENTS?
FWISH
AS LONG AS THEY AGREE!
SATURDAY OF THE FOLLOWING WEEK, 10:00 AM.
HE'S LATE!
BLUE SKY PARK.

HE SAID...
BE THERE AT 10 AM SHARP!
AND I WANT TO TAKE NATURAL PHOTOS, SO WEAR YOUR EVERYDAY CLOTHES. ♡
...DIDN'T HE?
SHINOBU-SAN, AREN'T THOSE CONSIDERED WORK CLOTHES?
IN MY OWN WAY, THIS IS NATURAL.
OH...
SORRY TO KEEP YOU WAITING!
AH, HERE HE COMES.
I APOLOGIZE! IT TOOK ME LONGER THAN I THOUGHT TO GET READY!
TA
TA
TA
TA
WELL, LET'S START. ♡
H...
GLITTER
SPANGLES
SPANGLES
SPANGLES
SPANGLES
GLITTER
HE'S DAZZLING...

UM... I DON'T MEAN TO BE RUDE...
BUT WON'T ALL THAT SPARKLY STUFF MESS UP THE PHOTOS?
OH, KEI-KUN!
DON'T YOU USE AN ASSISTANT?
NOPE. I DO THE WHOLE SHEBANG BY MYSELF.
HUH...
I DON'T GET THE CHANCE TO SHOOT HOT YOUNG MEN AND WOMEN EVERY DAY, YOU KNOW. THIS IS A SPECIAL OCCASION FOR ME, SO I WANTED TO SHOW YOU MY BEST OUTFIT!!
AS FOR MESSING UP THE PHOTOS?
YES, IT WOULD REFLECT ON THE LENS, UNFORTUNATELY...
RUSTLE
RUSTLE
SHIRT HE WORE OVER
SO HE DID THINK IT THROUGH...
ALL RIGHT,
...LET'S GO ONE AT A TIME FIRST...
...STARTING WITH OUR PRINCESS, TAKAMI-CHAN. ♡
EH?
AH... SURE...
PRACTICING HIS SMILE
KA
CHING
PRINCESS...?
GOOD LUCK!
SH-SHUT UP!!
ULP...
UHHH...
I-I'M NERVOUS...
GRIN...
L-LIKE THIS?
IT'S ALL RIGHT.
GRIN

YOU DON'T HAVE TO SMILE IF IT ISN'T COMFORTABLE.
BUT SHOW ME YOUR POWER.
EH?
TELL ME, "I'M A SUPERMODEL!"
"I'M THE HOTTEST WOMAN IN THE WORLD!" ♡
I CAN'T!!
YOU'RE BEAUTIFUL, TAKAMI-CHAN.
HUH?
...THAT'S STRANGE.
IT'S RIDICULOUS, BUT WHEN HE TELLS ME THAT...

FLASH
AN EXHIBITION...!
SHOULD I SMILE?
GRIN
FLASH
KYAAA! SHINOBU-SENSEI, YOU'RE SO HANDSOME. ♡
YESSS! I LOVE THE COOL LOOK!!
FLASH
...I FEEL LIKE I AM.
PRACTICING ...
...WAITING. ♡
OKAY.
UH... ...WHAT SHOULD I DO?
AND LAST BUT NOT LEAST,
AKIRA-KUN
THUMP THUMP
AKIRA!
MM... GOOD QUESTION.
SIT DOWN...
...WITH YOUR LEGS CROSSED...

LOOK THIS WAY...
...AND TRY TO MAKE IT SEXY.
FOO
SENSEI...
...IS THIS OKAY...?
FLASH
YES. PERFECT. ♡
NEXT, LOOK THE OTHER WAY.
OOO
FLASH

NO MATTER WHAT I SAY, HIS EXPRESSION STAYS THE SAME.
IT'S HARD TO BELIEVE HE'S A JUNIOR HIGH SCHOOL STUDENT.
I WANT TO TRY WIPING THAT PLACID LOOK OFF HIS FACE...
Replay
PFF
......
NEXT ....
...KEI-KUN AND TAKAMI-CHAN. ALL RIGHT?
EH?!
WHY DO I HAVE TO BE WITH KEI?!
YOU TOOK THE WORDS RIGHT OUTTA MY MOUTH!
WHAT ARE YOU TALKING ABOUT? YOU'RE THE ONLY MEMBER OF THE FAIRER SEX HERE...
...I'M GOING TO PAIR YOU UP WITH ALL OF THE MEN. ♡
Ah, actually there are two of us, but I have to take the photos...
EH...? AKIRA, I DON'T MIND, BUT...
...
I guess if we gotta, we gotta.
I'M LOOKING FORWARD TO THIS!
THAT'S RIGHT. GET A LITTLE CLOSER...
OH.

THIS WILL BE A WONDERFUL SHOT.
EH...?
WITH HIM? YUCK!
MY THOUGHTS EXACTLY!
CHUCKLE
CHUCKLE
FLASH
......
Rrrr...
YOU'RE BOTH TALL...
...SO IT'S AS IF YOU WERE MADE FOR EACH OTHER.
FLASH
AND NEXT UP, ODA-SENSEI.
I WANT THIS TO BE A SEXY SHOT, SO GRAB HER IN YOUR ARMS. ♡
WELL, REMEMBER, SHE IS MY STUDENT...
TAK
...SO I DON'T KNOW IF I SHOULD GRAPPLE HER.
TAK

RUSTLE
HEY...
FLASH
SQUEEZE
A-WEEEEE!!
IT'S NOT VERY PROFES-SIONAL...
YOU'RE DOING IT!! CAN'T GET ANY CLOSER THAN THAT!
EEEEEEK!
KYAAA!
AHAHAHAHAHAHA!
Check out that face!
KYAAAA!
FLASH
YOU LOOK LIKE A GENUINE COUPLE. ♡
Gosh, my stomach hurts...
BEAUTIFUL. ♡
FLASH
WILL YOU GET IN CLOSER TO EACH OTHER?
EH?
I DON'T SEE HOW WE CAN, WITHOUT...
......
SH
GASP
OVE
GRAB

HOW'S THIS?
A--
AKIRA?!
HMPH
FLASH
?
ADORABLE.
YOU LOOK LIKE BROTHER AND SISTER!
Ahaha
I KNOW, RIGHT?
RUFFLE RUFFLE
I'M REALLY PROUD OF MY LITTLE BROTHER!
BLUSH

PFFF
CUT IT!
PFFF...
CHUCKLE
I WAS RIGHT...
WELL...
...I'M SATISFIED HERE, SO SHALL WE GO TO THE STUDIO?
SATISFIED?
A PERSONAL JOKE.
WHAT CHANGES AKIRA-KUN'S EXPRES-SION...
ARE YOU GONNA TAKE MORE PICS IN THE STUDIO?
HUH? DIDN'T I TELL YOU?
FIRST I HEARD!
...IS TAKAMI-CHAN.
WELCOME ...
...TO MY WORKSHOP ♡
Wow... My first time in a studio?
COME ON IN.
AH...

A WHITE PIANO!
THAT'S SO COOL!
UH-HUH.
I KNEW YOU ALL PLAY,
SO I THOUGHT IT WOULD BE A NICE ACCOUTREMENT. IT'S A RENTAL...
HUH...
......
AKIRA SHOULD DO IT!
EH?
WHO MORE THAN AKIRA...
...IS SUITED FOR A BEAUTIFUL PURE WHITE PIANO LIKE THIS?!
T-TAKAMI...
SHOVE SHOVE
DEAR ME, YOU'RE RIGHT...

IT'S A NO-BRAINER!
WELL, THANKS, BUT...
HEEHEE
YESSS...
I'LL USE AKIRA-KUN FOR THE PIANO SHOT...
GIGGLE
...BUT I ALSO NEED YOU, TAKA-MI--CHAN.
EH?
30 MINUTES LATER
OH!
SHE'S READY...
LET'S GO, DARLING.
DRAG
HEY!
YA
ONE...
TWO...
I DON'T REALLY...
I DON'T...
NK
THREE!

WHOAAA...
......
TA-DAAA.
WHAT'S THE DEAL...?
LET'S PUT ON MAKEUP ♡
Aieeee!
HELD CAPTIVE FOR HALF AN HOUR
You never said anything about this!
I THOUGHT YOU WOULD MATCH THE PIANO THIS WAY. ♡

INCREDIBLE, TSUCHIYA-SAN.
A COMPLETE MAKEOVER IN 30 MINUTES?
IT'S LIKE THE OLD SAYING. "THE TAILOR MAKES THE MAN"... FIRST TIME I'VE SEEN IT PLAYED OUT IN REAL LIFE.
YOU TWO BETTER QUIT WHILE YOU'RE AHEAD...
STARE
HEE-HEE. OH, I'VE GOT AN INSATIABLE APPETITE FOR STUDYING VARIOUS THINGS. I EVEN MADE THIS DRESS. ♡
PRINCE...
...WOULD YOU HONOR THE PRINCESS BY PLAYING HER A PIECE OF MUSIC?
PLOP
EH?
AH...
...TH...
...THANK YOU.
Akira's gonna play the piano!
What's it gonna be? What's it gonna be?
...OF COURSE.

MARVELOUS. ♥
CHUCKLE
FLASH
TRICKLE
Dang, he's good...
GYMNOPEDIE NO. 1...
FLASH
HE'S GOT GOOD TASTE...

YOU CAN HAVE THESE, TO COMMEMORATE THE SHOOT ♡
HEH... THAT'S A GREAT SHOT... I HOPE YOU USE IT FOR YOUR SHOWING...
YOU GOTTA USE...
THIS SHOT OF ME AND AKIRA...!!
OF COURSE I'LL USE THEM. ♡
BUZZ
BUZZ
CHAK...

THAT'S A CUTE PHOTO, ISN'T IT? ♡
...WE REALLY DO LOOK LIKE BROTHER AND SISTER...
MMM... ADORABLE SIBLINGS. ♡
MUTTER
...I WONDER...
...IF I'LL ALWAYS BE THE LITTLE BROTHER...
HERE, AKIRA-KUN.
I'LL GIVE YOU THIS ONE.
THE BEST PHOTO I TOOK TODAY!
FWISH
EH...?

WHISPER
WHEN WE TOOK THIS...
...YOU LOOKED LIKE REAL LOVERS.
!!
HONEST.
...YOU'RE SURE...
...I CAN KEEP IT...?
NATURALLY.

I'LL TAKE GOOD CARE OF IT...
A JUNIOR HIGH SCHOOL STUDENT AFTER ALL...
The springtime of your life...
EH?
PRIVATE JOKE.
THANK YOU FOR EVERY-THING. ♡
NO, THANK *YOU*... ALL OF YOU. BE CAREFUL GOING HOME NOW.
BUZZ BUZZ
AKIRA, WHAT ARE YOU SMILING ABOUT?
PFFF
NOTH-ING...
YAWW-WN...
'M SLEEPY...
...SAY...
KEI-KUN...
YEAH?

WOW.
SQUEEZE
IT'S JUST THAT YOU'RE EXACTLY MY TYPE!!
KYAAA! I'M SORRY!!
SLAM!
Heh
YOU SHOULD SEE YOUR FACE RIGHT NOW! THAT'S WHAT YOU GET FOR LAUGHIN' AT PEOPLE!
AHA-HA-HA
LET'S GO HOME, TAKAMI.
YEAH ...
ASH

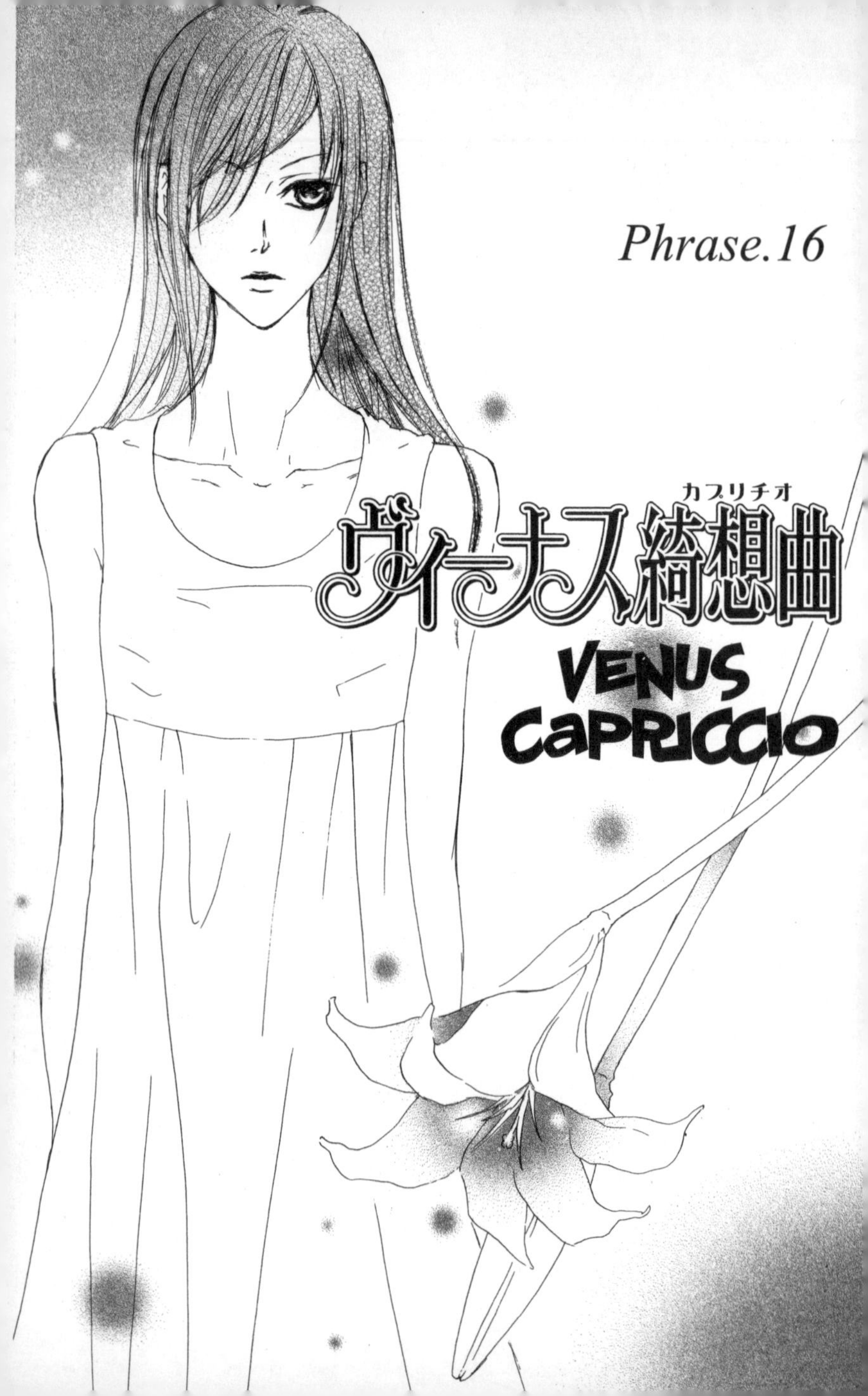
Phrase.16
カプリチオ
ヴィーナス綺想曲
VENUS
CAPRICCIO

THE NEW KITTEN

AT MY HOUSE

YOU LOOK PALE. ARE YOU...
TRICKLE...
YOU'RE SO SWEET...! AND CUTE AS A NEWBORN PUPPY...
SQUEEZE
I WISH YOU REALLY WERE MY LITTLE BROTHER...!!! DOCILE AS A LAMB...
EH?
WAIT... TAKAMI...
LET ME PRETEND YOU'RE MY BABY BROTHER!
TAKA-MI...
HEY...
I-I DON'T WANT TO BE YOUR LITTLE BROTHER...
TAKA-MI...
PLEASE, BABY BROTHER?!
T-TAKAMI!
WHAT HAPPENED?
DON'T ASK!
ONE HOUR EARLIER...
THE HABARA RESIDENCE.
DAIKI HABARA THE 4TH-OLDEST SON, 3RD-YEAR HIGH SCHOOL STUDENT.
TAKAMI...
T--
ARE YOU A MORON...?
HUH?
I'M HUNGRY! WHAT'S THE PROBLEM?

YOU SHOULD WAIT FOR DINNER TO START!!
WHEN YOU GET HUNGRY, YOU EAT. WHAT COULD BE SIMPLER?
CHEW CHEW
JUST OUT OF THE BATH
FWISH
Hmph. What do you mean, "moron", dummy?
FRIED CHICKEN
JUST 'CAUSE YOU'VE GOT FOUR BROTHERS...
...DOESN'T MEAN YOU HAVE TO ACT LIKE A MAN!!
COULD YOU TWO KEEP IT DOWN?
DON'T YOU HAVE ANY SENSE OF SHAME?!
ARE YOU REALLY A WOMAN?!
Takami, hurry up and get dressed.
MOM GOT A PERM
BITE ME. I'M GONNA GET DRESSED... SOON AS I FINISH EATING SOME CHICKEN...
GASP
...HEY, DON'T TELL ME...
...YOU PARADE AROUND HALF-NAKED LIKE THAT IN FRONT OF AKIRA?! LIKE AT HIS HOUSE...
EXCUSE ME?

THIS HAS NOTHING TO DO WITH AKIRA!
AND I SAY IT DOES! SO DO YOU?
CHAK
OF COURSE NOT!
YOU'RE UNBELIEVABLE!
AND YOU'RE A MENTAL MIDGET!
WHY DO YOU ALWAYS GOTTA HAVE THE LAST WORD?!
GYAAA
GYAAA
GYAAA
ARRRHHH
AND THEN HE SAID...
I WISH AKIRA WAS MY LITTLE SISTER!
YOU BELIEVE THAT?!
Die!
I don't need a sister like you!
I'M THE ONE WHO COULD USE A BROTHER LIKE YOU!! TICKS ME OFF!!
TAKAMI, CALM DOWN.
IT'S ME YOU'RE TALKING TO. IT'S OVER.
DON'T INTERRUPT ME!
AND THEN I'LL TAKE YOU HOME. BEFORE MIDNIGHT...

FOR-GET IT.
I REFUSE TO GO HOME UNTIL HE APOLOGIZES!!
GROWWWWWLLL
I'M STAYING HERE TONIG--
TONI--
GRRRRRR
GRRRRRR
GROWLLLLL
...D--
DID YOU... ALREADY-HAVE DINNER...?
BLUSH
IN THE KITCHEN
...NOT YET.
I WAS JUST STARTING TO MAKE IT.
Hah!
IS THAT RIGHT? OKAY, LEAVE IT TO ME!
THUD
THUD
YOUR BIG SISTER WILL MAKE SOMETHING TASTY!!
AH...
LIKE I WAS SAYING, I'M STAYING OVER TONIGHT!

5
LIKE I DID IN VENUS 2, HERE ARE A FEW MORE ROUGH SKETCHES OF MY LITTLE SISTER (HIGH SCHOOL STUDENT). BY THE WAY, SHE'S NOT ANYTHING LIKE ANY OF THE CHARACTERS IN VENUS. (I DID GET HER PERMISSION TO PUBLISH THESE SKETCHES OF HER, BUT WOULD'VE DONE IT EVEN IF SHE REFUSED.)
ERASING
DRAWING A STRAIGHT LINE
HOLDING A CAT
SORRY FOR THE STRANGE COLUMN
Oh. Just a lotta veg-etables?
Let's see, what should I make?
....
AH...
I'LL BRING HER HOME BEFORE IT GETS TOO LATE.
I FIGURED SHE'D GO TO YOUR HOUSE.
SORRY ABOUT THIS, AKIRA. THERE'S NO CALL FOR YOU TO GET INVOLVED IN OUR FAMILY DISPUTES.
THAT'S ALL RIGHT.
AH!

I...
I APOLOGIZE IN ADVANCE IF SHE DOES ANYTHING WEIRD...
? LIKE WHAT?
AH, NEVER MIND!!
W-WELL, I APPRECIATE THIS! BYE-BYE!
BYE.
KA-CHA
HEY! AKIRA!
YOU'RE OUT OF OIL! YOU GOT ANOTHER BOTTLE?
...
BE RIGHT THERE.
DANG!
THE OIL'S REALLY FLYING!
LOT MORE THAN USUAL...
CRACKLE CRACKLE
DID YOU PUT WATER IN THERE?
YEAH, A LITTLE...
UH-HUH...
GYAAA
!!
GYAAA
...ALL RIGHT.
Phew

MESS
HACKED-UP FRIED VEGETABLES
COMPLETE
BOILED RICE MIXED WITH HACKED-UP VEGETABLES
HACKED-UP VEGETABLE SOUP
HOW ABOUT THAT?!
YEAH, RIGHT?! EAT UP!!
CRUNCH
CRUNCH
CRUNCH
MUNCH MUNCH
AH...
DELICIOUS!
WHY...?
I always make this, but...
It's good.
......

HHHHH...
GOSH, I WISH I COULD SWITCH YOU AND DAIKI.
HOW
CUTE...
That jerk always makes fun of what I cook. He says it looks "inedible" and then he eats it. What the heck is that?
I SAID, I HAVE NO INTEREST IN BEING YOUR BROTHER.
HERE, PUT THESE LEFTOVERS IN THE FRIDGE.
DON'T WASH THIS.
OKAY.
TRI CKLE
A LITTLE BROTHER WHO HELPS CLEAR THE TABLE AND WASH THE DISHES...
INCREDIBLE...
DAIKI WOULD NEVER DO THAT...
SCRUB SCRUB
LALA LA
LALA LA
TAKA-MI...
AFTER WE'RE DONE CLEANING UP, I'LL TAKE YOU HO--
AH!
DANG! I FORGOT WRESTL-ING'S ON TONIGHT!

I'LL TAKE...
WHIZZZZ WHIZZZZ
HEY... TAKAMI...
ALL RIGHT! LET'S WATCH, AKIRA!
TAKA...
DRAG
WAAA
WAAA
YEAHHH! THERE IT IS!!
GRAB
THE SLEEPER HOLD!!
!
T...
TAKAMI, WHAT ARE YOU DOING?
WAAA
WAAA
YOU'RE HELPLESS!! AHAHAHA!
BLUSH
MUSH
MUSH
TA--

TAKAMI...
...COME ON, STOP IT...!
DO YOU GIVE UP?!
ULP...
YEAH. I GIVE UP, I GIVE UP.
OH, YEAHHH! I WIN!
......
THUMP
THUMP
GET 'IM!
HE'S WIDE OPEN!
AHHH...
......
TAKAMI...
IT'S ABOUT TIME I TAKE YOU HOME...
TIK
TIK
AHHH, THAT WAS FUN.
BUT I'M SWEATIN' LIKE A PIG.
FLAP
FLAP
AKIRA, LET ME USE YOUR BATH.
Hot in here

WHAT?!
YOU SERIOUSLY MEAN TO SPEND THE NIGHT...?!
ISN'T THAT WHAT I SAID?
I'M NOT GOING HOME UNTIL HE APOLOGIZES.
AH! I DIDN'T BRING ANY EXTRA CLOTHES, SO LET ME BORROW SOME OF YOURS.
SHORTS AND A T-SHIRT WILL BE FINE. *THANKS!*
I WON'T BE LONG!
TAKAMI...

...MAYBE YOU DON'T GET IT...
SO LET ME TELL YOU.
I...

YOU WHAT?
I...UM...
OH. YOU WANNA TAKE A BATH FIRST?
NO, THAT'S NOT IT...
ALL RIGHT, THEN I'LL GO.
WAI--

WAIT...
...A MINUTE!
FWISH
HEY, AKIRA!
WHAT'RE THESE?
TWITCH
RUSTLE
I SAID SHORTS AND A T-SHIRT!
Look how long this is...
THIS IS TOO HEAVY.
...PUT IT ON.
THEN I'M GOING TO TAKE YOU HOME.

HUH?
HOW MANY TIMES DID I TELL HIM I WASN'T GOING HOME?
COME ON, LET ME BORROW A PAIR OF SHORTS!
TUG TUG
EH?
HEY...
WHERE ARE WE GOING, TAKAMI?
YOUR ROOM, OF COURSE.
...MY ROOM?!
AND THEN LET'S PLAY SOME-THING!!
Hahaha! This can be like a slumber party!

CLIK
FLASH
MIND IF I OPEN YOUR CLOSET?
KA-CHA
CLIK
FOO
HEY!
WHUH...
OH. YOU DID THAT.
SCARED ME FOR A SECOND THERE.
I THOUGHT MAYBE IT WAS A BLACKOUT!

TA
TA
...?
WHAT...?
AKIRA, WHAT'S WRO--
I...
EH?
AKIRA...
EH?
...HUH?
WHAT'RE YOU TALKING ABOUT...?
...GAVE YOU PLENTY OF CHANCES TO LEAVE.
...IS HE MAD?
WHY...?
...WAKE UP.

BAM
BUMP
FWIP

FWAP
...AT NIGHT, YOU GO TO THE HOUSE...
...OF A GUY WHO LIVES ALONE?
YOU NEED TO USE MORE COMMON SENSE.
...DO YOU HAVE ANY IDEA...
...HOW I FEEL ABOUT YOU...?
NOT JUST TODAY.
SINCE WE FIRST MET.
I'M NOT YOUR LITTLE BROTHER.
IF YOU CAN'T UNDER-STAND THAT...

FWISH
TWITCH
...LET ME MAKE IT CLEAR.

THUMP
SQUEEZE
THUMP
THUMP
THUMP
WHUMP

...OW...
...

GASP
...
AH!
S-SORR--
...Y...
UH... I THINK...
...I'LL GO HOME AFTER ALL!
TA TA
KA-CHA
SLAM
TA TA TA
TA TA

...OHHH...
FWUMP
...GOD.
......
IT'S YOUR FAULT, TAKAMI...

301
HABARA
SLAM
TA TA TA TA TA...
MM?
KA-CHA
AHAHAHA. SO YOU BROKE DOWN IN THE END AND CAME HOME, HUH?
DOPE!
TA TA
TA TA TA
TA
DID YOU COOL OFF?
SHUT YOUR FRIGGIN' MOUTH!!
SLAM
...YEESH. WHAT'S WITH HER?
SHE PROBABLY REALIZED HOW FOOLISH...
...SHE WAS.
WHO, THAT IDIOT?
HOW WOULD SHE NOTICE?
YOU'RE AN IDIOT, TOO.
EH...?
It's true.

DUN
DUN
DUN
DUN
DUN
DUN
......!!
M-MY HEART...!!
THUMP
"LITTLE BROTHER..."

"I'M THE ONE WHO COULD USE A BROTHER LIKE YOU!!"
"I WISH YOU REALLY WERE MY LITTLE BROTHER...!!!"
"I'M REALLY PROUD OF MY LITTLE BROTHER!"

THUMP
"...LITTLE BROTHER"...?
"IF YOU CAN'T UNDER-STAND THAT, LET ME MAKE IT CLEAR."
THUMP
NO, HE'S NOT.

IT SEEMS LIKE...
...HE'S A MAN THAT I DIDN'T KNOW...

カプリチオ
ヴィーナス綺想曲
VENUS Capriccio
Phrase.17

GLOOOM
SIGH...
SIGHHH...
DID SOMETHING HAPPEN WITH AKIRA LAST WEEK?
RATTLE
AH!
HAH?!
H-HOW'D YOU KNOW...?

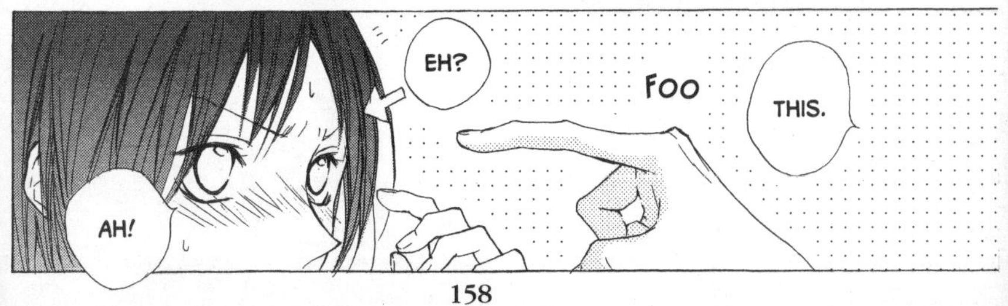
THIS.
FOO
EH?
AH!

SINCE LAST WEEK, YOU'VE BEEN PLAYING WITH THAT FACE.
SINCE LAST WEEK, YOU HAVEN'T BEEN COMING TO YOUR LESSON WITH AKIRA.
WHAT OTHER CONCLU-SION IS THERE?
W--
WELL, YOU'RE WRONG!!
BAM!
AND OUR TIME'S UP, SO I'M GOING HOME.
KACHA
Hmph
...AH...
KA-CHA

TAKA--
AKIRA, LET'S HIT IT!
THUD
OH, TAKAMI, YOU'RE DONE, TOO? *MY LESSON JUST FINISHED.*
THUD
LET'S ALL GO HOME TOGETHER.
LATELY, HE'S BEEN LEAVING WITH AKIRA.
BAM
KA
CHA
WHAT, DID YOU FORGET SOME-THING?
HEY! DON'T OPEN THE DOOR!

Huh?
WHAT'S UP?
TAK...
...
GASP
FWISH
WHUH...?!
WHAT?!
RATTLE
WHAT'S HER DEAL? SHE WAS LIKE THIS LAST WEEK, TOO.
....
SHIVER
SHIVER
ISN'T THIS...
...A LITTLE TOO CLOSE?
TAK
HUH?
HEY, TAKAMI, AREN'T YOU GONNA GO...?
TAK...
TAK...

TAK
TAK
...HEY.
YOU GUYS ARE ACTIN' WEIRD.
PAT
DID SOMETHING HAPPEN BETWEEN...
...?
What's wrong?
NOTHING.
...NEVER MIND.

...
TAKAMI, WE'RE LEAVING WITHOUT YOU!
YANK
?!
TAK
TAK
H-HEY, AZEGAMI, WHAT ARE YOU DOING...?
WE'RE GOING.
G-GOING WHERE...?
JUST COME ON!
RUMBLE
RUMBLE
AOYAMA PIANO SCHOOL
AOYAMA PIANO SCHOOL
....
YOU'RE OKAY WITH THEM LEAVING BEFORE YOU?
GASP
O--
OF COURSE! WHY WOULDN'T I BE?! I'M NOT A CHILD!
STARE
WHAT...?
...

IF YOU WANNA TALK, I'LL LISTEN.
...I...
I JUST DON'T KNOW...
KNOW WHAT?
I KEEP THINKING ABOUT AKIRA...
...A-AND MY HEART WON'T STOP RACING.
...B-BUT I DON'T KNOW...
...HOW TO TALK TO HIM.

BLUSH
FSSS
Eh? Who are you?
AH, BOYS...
MOVED
YEAH, BUT SEE ...
...HE'S LIKE A LITTLE BROTHER TO ME, SO...
HUH...
SO HE NEARLY KISSED YOU.
NEARLY ...
RUMBLE RUMBLE...
...LITTLE BROTHER?
...U-UH-HUH.
S-SO I WANNA BE ABLE TO TALK TO HIM NORMALLY AGAIN, LIKE HOW WE WERE BEFORE, BUT...
YOU'RE SPEAKING FRANKLY?
EH...?
AKIRA'S YOUR "LITTLE BROTHER."
YOU ALWAYS SAY THAT...
...BUT IT THATS TRUE...
WHY CAN'T YOU STOP THINKING ABOUT HIM?

RATTLE
HEH.
EH? W-WELL...
POOR AKIRA.
...BECAUSE OF WHAT HAPPENED. ANYBODY WOULD...
CREAK
IT'S ABOUT TIME YOU OPENED YOUR EYES.

ZAAAA
RAMEN
RAMEN
CLINK
AZEGAMI...
WHY DO I HAVE TO BE HERE EATING RAMEN WITH YOU?
IT'S STARTED TO RAIN AND I WANNA GO HOME...
IT'S NOT ABOUT EATING, JERK!
BUZZ
BUZZ BUZZ
"JERK" ...?
BUZZ
A BOWL OF MISO!
SOMETHING HAPPENED BETWEEN YOU AND TAKAMI, RIGHT?
TELL ME ABOUT IT!
...WHY WOULD I TELL YOU...
HEY, HEY, DON'T UNDERESTIMATE ME HERE.
FWI!
TRUST IN THE GUY WHO'S BEEN CALLED...
"MEISHIN JUNIOR HIGH'S MINISTER OF LOVE"!!
SSH!
CLAK

CHAK
AH!
THE WATER...
...IS GOING RIGHT BETWEEN MY LEGS!!
SIR, IS EVERYTHING ALRIGHT?
AH! S-SORRY...
Oooh...
....
STUPID...
N-NEVER MIND THIS! W-WE'RE NOT LEAVIN' 'TIL YOU TELL ME WHAT'S GOING ON!!
GOT IT?!
...FINE.
BUT DO YOU HAVE TO BE SO NOISY ABOUT IT...?
WH-WHO YOU CALLIN' NOISY?!
YOU ARE.
6
WELL, THIS IS THE LAST COLUMN.
THEY LET ME DO ANOTHER BONUS MANGA, ETC. AT THE END OF THIS VOLUME, TOO.
CHECK IT OUT OF YOU GET THE CHANCE.
THANK YOU FOR STICKING WITH ME ALL THIS WAY.
SO LONG FOR NOW.
THIS HAS BEEN MAI NISHIKATA.

30 MINUTES LATER...
ZAAAA
EH...?
Y-YOU TOLD HER HOW YOU FELT ABOUT HER, YOU KISSED HER BEFORE...
AND SO YOU TRIED ATTACKING HER...?
DON'T MAKE IT LIKE A LIST!!
I'm not checking things off as I go!
BLUSH
FINALLY SPEAKING, AFTER 30 MINUTES
AH.
OKAY, SORRY.
But it is like a list...
UM... ALL RIGHT.
...YEAH.
I CAN SEE HOW YOU'D BE IMPATIENT...
IF YOU HADN'T GONE THAT FAR, SHE'D PROBABLY BE REFERRING TO YOU AS HER "LITTLE BROTHER" 'TIL KINGDOM COME...
...THAT'S IT.
MM?
...I TOLD YOU EVERYTHING.
THERE ISN'T ANYTHING ELSE TO SAY...
OH...
I'M GOING HOME.
RATTLE
AH!!

WAIT!
WE WERE JUST GETTING TO THE NITTY GRITTY!
GRAB
THE NITTY GRITTY?
HUH?
YEAH! I MEAN, WHAT, YOU WANNA TAKE OFF RIGHT AFTER YOU TELL ME THE PROBLEM?
SORRY... I'VE NEVER TALKED TO ANYONE...
...ABOUT THIS KIND OF THING BEFORE...
...I, UH...
WELCOME!
BUZZ
BUZZ
I'M OUT OF MY ELEMENT HERE...
HUH?
DASH
OKAY! WAIT! WAIT!
SORRY! I DIDN'T KNOW...
LIKE I SAID, LEAVE IT TO THE "MINISTER OF LOVE"!
HERE'S WHAT YOU GOTTA DO...
PLOP

UM...
...ER...
F-FIRST...
APOLOGIZE TO HER, I THINK...
TH-THEN, I GUESS, ASK HER OUT ON A DATE...
THIS, UH...
SEQUENCE OF ACTIONS IS VERY IMPORTANT...
AFTER ALL, SHE IS...
...A WOMAN.
BUZZ
BUZZ
RATTLE

...THANKS,
AZEGAMI.
I'M GONNA APOLOGIZE TO HER!
COOL...
I DIDN'T KNOW HE WAS SO PURE...
Good luck!
Hmph
This kind of image
esson room 1

HUFF
HUFF
THAT REALLY HURT...
KOFF KOFF...
KICKED IN THE STOMACH
...HOW ABOUT A SOCK ON THE JAW FOR A FOLLOW-UP?
HUFF
HUFF
Ooogh...
...YOU'RE NOT INTERESTED?
RUMBLE
OF COURSE NOT!
WHAT?! LIKE I'D BE INTO SEXUAL HARASS-MENT?!
RUMBLE
RUMBLE
* ONLY AT-TEMPTED, JUST IN CASE...
HAH?!
WHAT ABOUT WHEN YOU WERE WITH AKIRA?
WHAT DID YOU THINK WHEN HE TRIED TO STEAL A KISS?

WHEN AKIRA TRIED TO...?
AKI--
BAM
BUMP
THUMP
I WASN'T...
I...
I WAS CAUGHT OFF...
...GUARD.
THUMP
I MEAN...
I DIDN'T...
THUMP

I...
...DIDN'T...
...MIND.
GRIN
FWISH
...AND THERE'S YOUR ANSWER.
HOW MANY TIMES...
ZAAAA
SPLISH
SPLISH

RUFFLE RUFFLE
SQUEEZE
"I'M REALLY PROUD OF MY LITTLE BROTHER!"
"I WISH YOU REALLY WERE MY LITTLE BROTHER...!!!"
...WITHOUT EVEN THINKING ABOUT...
SPLISH
...HAVE I CALLED HIM...
SPLISH
...MY "LITTLE BROTHER" UP TO NOW?
...HOW HE FELT...
...WHILE HE WAS BESIDE ME...
AKIRA!

ALL THIS TIME.
AKIRA, I'M SORRY!
I...
AT YOUR HOUSE, I WASN'T THINK-ING...
AND NOT ONLY THEN...
A-ALL THIS TIME...
...I HAVEN'T BEEN GIVING ANY THOUGHT...
What the...?
STARE

TO THE WAY YOU FEE--
Y--
YOU'RE SHOUTING, TAKAMI.
CLANG
CLANG
CLANG
SPLISH
ZAAAA
....
I'M THE ONE...
...THAT NEEDS TO APOLOGIZE.

...I-IT'S REALLY COMIN' DOWN, AKIRA...
Y--
YOU'VE GOT A FOLDING UMBRELLA, DON'T YOU? LIKE ALWAYS...
I...
I FORGOT IT...
SIMPLE RECONCILIATION
ZAAAAA
...
...IT'S...
...IT'S OKAY.
...TH-THEN, C'MON. YOU CAN GET UNDER MINE! IT'S REALLY SHINOBU-SENSEI'S, BUT...
TAKAMI...
CAN I ASK YOU ONE THING...?
...HUH?
TO YOU...
ZAAAA
...AM I STILL...

...A LITTLE
BROTHER?

ZAAAAAAA
L--
LET'S GO HOME, AKI...
SPLISH
TAKAMI.
...HEY.
...COME ON, TAKAMI...
....
THUMP
THUMP
...TELL HIM.
THUMP
TELL HIM.

TELL HIM!
...NO.
NO!

PAT
PAT
...TAKA--
LET'S
LET'S GO.
YOU'LL CATCH COLD.
...IS THAT THE TRUTH?
......
WH--
WHAT WOULD BE THE POINT...
...OF LYING?

BUMP

...GOOD.
...HEY...

W-WHAT'RE YOU DOIN'...?
...YOU DON'T LIKE IT?
IT'S NOT THAT I DON'T LIKE IT, BUT...
THEN I WON'T STOP.
SQUEEZE
SQUEEZE
YOUR ...
...ARMS ARE COLD...!
VENUS CAPRICCIO (3): THE END

BONUS PAGES

BONUS MANGA
REPLACE
WHAT IF TAKAMI AND AKIRA SWITCHED PERSONALITIES?
PART THREE
Zzzzz
AKIRA...
DO YOU WANT TO TAKE HOME THE LEFTOVER MEAT?
AKIRA.
MMM...
I WON THE MEAT...
CHUCKLE
...AKIRA, IF YOU'RE SLEEPY, YOU CAN BORROW A BEDROOM.
YES, I KNOW...
GO AHEAD AND TAKE A NAP.
FOO
AKIRA, COME ON...
...TAKAMI ALWAYS...
...TREATS ME LIKE A CHILD.

GRAB
I'M...
WAKE...
...NOT A CHILD.
...CUT IT OUT.
YOU'RE HALF ASLEEP, SO NOW WAKE UP THE OTHER HALF!
AKIRA-KUN...
I'M NOT...
SQUEEZE
YEESH...
...A CHILD.
TO BE CONTINUED...

KEI AZEGAMI
HEIGHT 5'10"
USUALLY WEARS JERSEYS.
I THINK OF HIM AS A PRETTY AVERAGE BOY.
IT'S EASY TO DRAW HIM IN A VARIETY OF DIFFERENT SITUATIONS.

AFTERWORD

THANK YOU FOR READING THIS FAR!

I REGRET VARIOUS THINGS ABOUT THIS THIRD VOLUME (ALTHOUGH I ALWAYS FEEL THAT WAY), BUT I'M REALLY HAPPY THAT IT'S COMPLETE AND HAS SAFELY ARRIVED IN YOUR HANDS.

IT'S ALL THANKS TO YOU, THE PEOPLE WHO HAVE READ THIS; WHO SUPPORT ME; WHO WRITE LETTERS AND OTHERWISE ENCOURAGE ME.

THANK YOU VERY MUCH!!

SPECIAL THANKS TO:

MY EDITOR, S-SAMA; RYU KUGA-SAMA; ERIRIN OKUYAMA; AIPU; TSUKUDA-SENSEI; NAKAZAWA-SAN

ALL OF MY FRIENDS AND PEOPLE I KNOW WHO SUPPORTED ME
MY DEAR FAMILY
AND EVERYONE WHO PLAYED A PART IN GETTING THIS BOOK PUBLISHED

IF YOU HAVE ANY THOUGHTS, OPINIONS, ETC. YOU'D LIKE TO SHARE ABOUT THIS TITLE, PLEASE SEND THEM TO ME AT:

MAI NISHIKATA/VENUS CAPRICCIO
C/O CMX
888 PROSPECT STREET
SUITE 240
LA JOLLA,
CA 92037

AND ON THAT NOTE, I HOPE WE MEET AGAIN IN THE PAGES OF VOLUME 4!
THIS HAS BEEN NISHIKATA. NOVEMBER, 2007.

BONUS PAGES: THE END

Sheldon Drzka	Translation and Adaptation
MPS Ad Studio	Lettering
Larry Berry	Art Directo
Chynna Clugston Flores	Assistant E
Jim Chadwick	Editor

Jim Lee	Editorial Di
Hank Kanalz	VP—Gener
Paul Levitz	President &
Richard Bruning	SVP—Crea
Patrick Caldon	EVP—Finan
Amy Genkins	SVP—Business & Legal Affairs
Gregory Noveck	SVP—Creative Affairs
Steve Rotterdam	SVP—Sales & Marketing
Cheryl Rubin	SVP—Brand Management